CALHOUN'S BOUNTY

With his dying breath, a bullet-ridden man staggers into Stonewall's saloon clutching a gold bar, and names bounty hunter Denver Calhoun as his killer. Despite the dead man being one of the bank-raiding Flynn gang, the hunt is on for Denver. In Bluff Creek, when the unlikely Horace Turner wagers a gold bar in a poker game, Denver reckons that the Flynns are involved. Can he succeed in bringing them to justice though, now the bounty hunter has become the hunted?

I. J. PARNHAM

CALHOUN'S BOUNTY

Complete and Unabridged

LINFORD
Leicester

First published in Great Britain in 2006 by
Robert Hale Limited
London

First Linford Edition
published 2007
by arrangement with
Robert Hale Limited
London

The moral right of the author has been asserted

British Library CIP Data

Parnham, I. J.
    Calhoun's bounty.—Large print ed.—
Linford western library
    1. Western stories
    2. Large type books
    I. Title
    823.9'2 [F]

ISBN 978–1–84617–702–6

Published by
F. A. Thorpe (Publishing)
Anstey, Leicestershire

Set by Words & Graphics Ltd.
Anstey, Leicestershire
Printed and bound in Great Britain by
T. J. International Ltd., Padstow, Cornwall

This book is printed on acid-free paper

Prologue

Deputy Luther Miles paced carefully into the wrecked shell of Bent Knee's bank. With his arms held above his head to shield himself from any masonry that might fall, he surveyed the damage.

The Flynn gang had been thorough.

Two hours ago they'd roared into town and charged straight into the bank. In their usual efficient way they hadn't wasted time or given anyone a chance to fight back.

Four masked men had held the tellers and customers at gunpoint while two others lassoed the safe. Heavy bolts had secured the safe to the floor and back wall, but dynamite had soon dislodged it. Then, while a four-horse team had dragged the safe out of town, they'd spread confusion by throwing more dynamite into the bank then fleeing, giving everyone inside just seconds to run for their lives.

Now the bank building, the oldest standing structure in town, was a crumbling shell.

'You reckon we can salvage anything?' Blaine Hobbs, the head teller, asked as he climbed over the rubble to join the deputy sheriff.

'Nope,' Luther said looking up at what had been the bank's back wall and which had been reduced to a single finger of teetering stone. 'Let's get out of here. This place ain't safe.'

Blaine nodded and the two men picked a route out of the wrecked bank, avoiding getting too close to the walls. Then a terrible creak sounded and then a grinding.

Luther and Blaine darted their gazes around, desperately searching for which wall was about to collapse, but it was the floor that shook. Then a ten-foot-square section that had once been the bank's central flagstone broke in two and dropped away.

A huge plume of dust burst out of the hole as the two men backed away, glancing around them as they dreaded the collapse of the entire building. But the rumbling subsided and, with a relieved glance at each other, Luther then Blaine shuffled past the hole.

Luther waded through the swirling dust and reached the stark outline of what had once been the bank's front door, then he glanced back to urge Blaine to hurry. He couldn't see him. He narrowed his eyes as he peered into the dust, finally locating Blaine's outline kneeling beside the new hole in the floor.

'Come on, Blaine,' he urged. 'This whole building could collapse.'

'It could,' Blaine said, his voice wistful, 'but you got to come see this.'

Luther rocked back and forth on his heels, but then decided that the quickest way of persuading Blaine to leave was to see what had interested him.

'This had better be good,' he

grumbled as he headed back to him.

'It sure is. There's a whole room under here I never knew existed. I'm guessing nobody has seen down here in twenty years.'

'That don't interest me,' Luther snapped as he hunkered down beside Blaine on the edge of the hole.

'Me neither, but what's in it does.'

Luther snorted his disbelief that this would be true, but as a stray beam of sunlight sliced through the dust and illuminated the room below, that sunlight reflecting back with twice the intensity, Luther's mouth fell open.

For a full minute both men stared down through the hole in the ruined bank floor, transfixed. Luther was the first to speak.

'Now,' he said, his voice emerging as a croaked whisper. 'What are we going to do about this?'

1

Five seconds after Denver Calhoun had kicked open the door two men lay dying, and the other three already had one foot in Boot Hill.

Denver dropped the third man with a high shot to the chest that wheeled him into the wall before he slid to the floor. The fourth man was sitting at a table on which a gold bar lay and he wasted valuable seconds grabbing the bar before jumping to his feet, but Denver hammered lead into his guts. The force kicked the man backward through the window, his arms splayed, a flash of gold following him as he tumbled outside.

And that left one man skulking behind the table.

'Come out with those hands reaching for heaven,' Denver ordered, 'and you won't go to hell.'

'I ain't listening,' the man shouted from behind the table.

Denver paced sideways, crossing his legs over each other as he gained a better angle on his quarry. He had followed this errant strand of Flynn's outlaw gang to this remote house midway between Stonewall and Bluff Creek. Even though he didn't expect rich pickings from their bounty, he still hoped that they might lead him to Flynn.

But he'd only do that if he took this last man alive.

'I only want Flynn. Tell me where he is and you'll live.'

The man snorted his lack of interest in Denver's offer, then leapt up, his gun swinging down to level on him, but before he could loose off a shot, Denver tore lead into his chest, bending him double. And a second shot to the head spun him to the floor.

As he reloaded Denver heard breathing nearby, the sound grating through the silence that had descended on the room, He darted his gaze across the dead outlaws until it rested on one man who lay sprawled, clutching his chest. He was the first man Denver had shot after bursting through the door and, in the confusion, it was possible he'd only winged him.

Denver paced to him, glancing left and right from the corners of his eyes as he confirmed that the other men in the room were in fact dead, then loomed over the man.

'Name?' he said, kicking his gun away.

'Rico, Rico Warren,' the man murmured, his eyes closed, his breath short and tortured. 'This is just my house. I wasn't with them. I wasn't . . . '

Rico uttered a pained gasp. His back arched and his head rocked to the side, but when he slumped to lie flat, he was still breathing. So Denver hunkered down beside him. He glanced at the reddened bullet-hole in his shirt, then ran the end of his gun barrel over Rico's forehead.

'Here's how it works, Rico. I don't care what you did or didn't do. I just want the bounty on your ugly hide. So, you can save your excuses for the law, but if you try anything, you won't get the chance to tell no stories. Understand?'

Rico murmured, his ill-formed words and pained delivery suggesting he wasn't in a fit state to try anything even if he wanted to.

Denver stood, then dragged the other bodies to the door as he prepared to take them to the outlaws' wagon, but all the time watching the supine Rico. Then he backed away to the window to peer outside.

He'd blasted one outlaw through the window, hitting him full in the guts, and that man ought to be lying beneath the window, but when he looked outside the area was deserted. A trail of blood snaked away.

Denver winced and darted back from the window to press himself to the wall, silently cursing himself for not having checked on this man first.

In the centre of the room, the barely conscious Rico sniggered to himself.

★ ★ ★

The wagon rider was clearly determined to go to hell.

The Turner brothers, Jack, Emmet and Horace, watched the wagon hurtle along the treacherous edge of Broken Rock Canyon at breakneck speed, its speeding form dark against the deep-blue sky beyond. None of them could believe what he was seeing.

They had been riding towards Bluff Creek along the bottom of the canyon, skirting around the snaking path of the river with their horses piled high with furs, when they'd heard shooting echoing back and forth between the canyon walls. And that was when the wagon had hurtled into view.

There was a sole rider. Trailing behind were five other riders; these men were trading gunfire with a sprawling group of around twenty chasing men.

'He's too near the side,' Emmet said, holding a hand to his brow to shield his eyes from the high sun.

'And he's going too fast,' Jack said.

But it was Horace who pointed out the worst danger.

'Any idiot riding that close to the edge and that fast can't know the area. And he won't know what's ahead.'

All three men winced then dragged their horses around and hurried back along their former route, trying to keep pace with the wagon above. About a half-mile on was a crumbling stretch of land where the earth was wont to fall away and slide to the bottom of the canyon. It had claimed more than one newcomer to the area. So, as they hurried to keep level with the wagon, they hollered, but the wagon rider was over 800 feet higher than they were. And he didn't even glance down.

'What you reckon this chase is about?' Jack shouted to the others, when yet another echoing shout had failed to gain a response.

Neither man offered a suggestion and, with the wagon trundling closer to the dangerous section of the canyon side, they redoubled their shouting. But they were too late.

Jack saw a stretch of earth bulge. Then a ten-yard length of the canyon side fell away beneath the horses' hoofs. One horse reared and the other stumbled, but the wagon almost made it to safety, the driver having the sense to urge the horses to keep going. But the wagon's momentum couldn't defeat the pull of gravity and it ground to a halt with one back wheel spinning in the air and the other mired in shifting dirt.

And with tragic inevitability, the wagon slipped backwards, slowly at first then gathering speed until it tipped over and came sliding down the side of the almost sheer canyon.

Below, the Turner brothers watched in horror as the horses, man and wagon tumbled end over end towards them.

Jack saw the driver roll free before the wagon broke in two half-way down, but by then he'd stopped hoping that the driver would survive.

He looked to the top of the canyon. The wagon's accompanying riders had stopped to confirm they could do nothing to help him, then they had hurried on, but the following riders split into two. One group stayed to watch the wagon tumble and the others headed off to pursue the men.

At the bottom of the canyon the largest section of the wagon came to a rattling halt in a cloud of dust. The other piece tumbled on for another fifty yards; the horses and driver skidded to a halt further up the slope.

Jack and Emmet dismounted and hurried to the driver's side, but long before they reached him Jack saw that they could do nothing for him. The body lay broken with its back and limbs twisted into angles no living man could ever have. Jack winced and looked up, but they were in a hollow and so the men at the top of the canyon were out of sight.

'It'll take a while for them to get down here,' Emmet said.

Jack nodded. The entrance to Broken Rock Canyon was twenty miles away, although there was a downward route ten miles back that wasn't well known and which crossed back and forth along the sides of a treacherous pass. He was pondering how he could trade signals with the men above to find out whether they knew about this route when Horace shouted for them to join him.

They headed down the slope past two spinning wheels and several broken planks. Beyond the remainder of the wrecked wagon Horace was sitting in front of a metal box that had rolled clear, and he'd prised open the top to peer inside.

'What you found in there?' Jack asked.

Horace looked up, his eyes wide and shocked, a glow rippling across his cheeks.

'You just got to see for yourself,' he

13

said, his voice catching in his throat.

Jack and Emmet exchanged a bemused glance, then both men looked over his shoulders and into the box. Low whistles escaped their lips.

'Gold,' Emmet murmured, his breath coming in short gasps.

'And plenty of it,' Horace said, sitting back. The high sun blasted off the tops of the rows and rows of gold bars inside and lit up all three men's faces with enticing ripples of golden sunlight.

'There's got to be a hundred bars in there,' Jack said.

'Maybe more,' Horace said. A finger darted between each bar as he mouthed numbers to himself.

'And how much is that worth?' Emmet murmured.

Jack gulped. 'Don't know, but it's safe to say a hell of a lot.'

Jack, Emmet, and Horace all nodded and, as one, their gazes rose to look up the canyon-side. Neither the chasing nor the pursuing men at the top were visible.

'You reckon they know about that quick route down here?' Horace said.

'Might do, might not,' Emmet said, 'but either way, I reckon it'll take them a while to get down here and claim their gold.'

All three brothers chuckled.

★ ★ ★

The man looked to be half-dead as he staggered into Stonewall's only saloon.

By the bar, Sheriff Mitchell stared at him agog, the other customers matching his surprise.

The man stood stooped before the swinging batwings, a gun dangling from a slack hand, his other hand clutching his guts. And from the bright blood oozing between his splayed fingers and dripping to the floor, that hand was probably keeping him intact.

He staggered a pace towards the bar, leaving behind a pool of blood and, as if that motion broke everyone out of their spells of shock, two men hurried to help him. But the man saw them coming and straightened up, then aimed his gun in their general direction.

The barrel was shaking so much that Sheriff Mitchell doubted he could hit anyone, but the approaching men had the sense to back away with their hands held high in calming and placating gestures.

The man sneered at them, then wended a snaking path across the saloon. He clattered to a halt when he stumbled into the bar.

'Whiskey,' he grunted, slamming his gun on the counter.

The barkeep poured him a full measure and the man released his weapon to grab the glass, then throw it down his throat. He grimaced then slammed the glass back on the counter and signified he wanted another one.

With the other customers giving him a wide berth, Mitchell headed down the bar to stand beside him. He noted that the injured man had placed his gun on the counter, but that his hand never strayed far from it. Mitchell kept his hand loose and dangling beside his holster.

'You seen some trouble,' he said.

The man glanced at him from the corner of his eye, then knocked back his second whiskey.

'You're mighty observant for a lawman,' he murmured through gritted teeth, then swiped a layer of sweat from his brow.

'You want to tell me who did it?'

'Nope.'

'Can't arrest him unless you give me a name.'

'I'll deal with it,' the man grunted, then spat to the side, the phlegm streaked with red.

Mitchell shrugged. 'And there was me thinking you wanted to stand there bleeding to death rather than get the man who shot you.'

'You want me to talk, is that it?'

'Won't learn nothing if you don't.' Mitchell threw a dollar on the bar.

'Here's what we'll do. I'll pay for your drinks, you and me will sit down and have ourselves a talk, and someone will get you some help.'

'Don't want no help. Don't want no talk.' The man snorted, the sound somewhere between grim humour and terminal despair. 'And I'll pay.'

The man reached into his pocket and, when his hand emerged, he clutched a gold bar. The light shining off it sprinkled around the saloon and generated a long intake of breath.

'Where you get that?' Mitchell asked.

The man slammed the gold bar on the counter.

'Barkeep,' he grunted, 'keep the whiskey coming until I've spent it.'

With his eyes wide and fixed on the gold, the barkeep filled another glass. The man reached for it, but his hand shook and when he grabbed the glass, it slipped from his hand and scooted off the counter to crash to the floor. The man followed the glass, his clawed hand holding on to the counter a moment

18

before he folded and fell.

The customers edged in towards him, as Mitchell knelt, then turned him over. The man lay with his pain-racked limbs twitching, his breath coming in short gasps.

'A name?' Mitchell asked.

A bubbling gasp escaped the dying man's lips and Mitchell reckoned he wouldn't answer, but then it came.

'Denver Calhoun,' he breathed. Then he didn't breathe again.

Mitchell stood, and already the customers were eyeing the gold bar on the counter with far more interest than they were eyeing the dead man.

'How much you reckon it's worth?' one man asked.

'Plenty,' another said. 'But who owns it now?'

More questions came, but Mitchell raised his hands, calling for calm.

'The answer to all those questions is simple.' He took the gold bar from the counter and held it aloft, letting everyone get a proper look at the gold.

'Whoever brings in Denver Calhoun gets this here gold bar.'

Despite the lure of looking at the gold, within a minute the saloon was deserted.

2

'We shouldn't have taken it,' Jack Turner said.

'We know that,' Horace said, 'but it don't change the fact we have.'

The last hour had passed as if it were a dream. Before they'd seen the wagon the Turner brothers had been heading through Broken Rock Canyon to Bluff Creek to trade the furs they'd caught over the last two months. They had been looking forward to a wild night of fun before buying the provisions that'd see them through to the next time they had to head into town.

But then they'd found more gold than any of them ever expected to see, perhaps more than any man ever expected to see.

They knew Broken Rock Canyon well and had forded the river and headed up a snaking pass that got them out on to the plains quickly. They'd covered their tracks, but to appear less suspicious they'd travelled at a steady rate and had now stopped on the edge of a ridge where they could see anyone approaching from the canyon.

Down below was a lake, a pine-coated slope stretching up to meet them, and some thirty miles on was Bluff Creek.

So far, the consequences of what they'd done had yet to hit them.

'We got to ask ourselves one question,' Jack said. 'Whose gold have we taken?'

'I guess,' Emmet said, shrugging, 'we won't find that out until we get to Bluff Creek.'

'And when we do, we'll find out that somebody wants it back mighty bad, whether that be the men chasing after it, or the men being chased.' Jack looked at each of his brothers in turn, receiving nods as the dangers that either group of men represented sank in. 'So, I reckon we got to do the right thing and hand this gold in.'

'I guess you're right,' Emmet said, his tone reluctant. 'But there's a whole heap of gold here. Perhaps they won't miss one bar.'

'Or three,' Horace said.

'Yeah,' Emmet said, brightening, 'one bar apiece ought to be enough for us to enjoy ourselves without getting into trouble.'

'I kind of figured we were enjoying ourselves before,' Jack said as Emmet and Horace looked at him for support. 'What's the likes of us going to do with a gold bar?'

Emmet lowered his head and Jack reckoned that Horace would agree, but to his disappointment, Horace shook his head.

'Not as much as we could do with a hundred gold bars,' he said.

Emmet raised his head to grunt his agreement and, unable to think of an immediate retort, Jack looked away to stare down at the lake, sighing.

After the initial excitement of discovering

the gold, when Jack had been as eager as his younger brothers to steal it, he'd reconsidered. He now wished they could pretend they'd never found it and so return to their former plan of riding into town, trading furs, and having a wild and drunken night.

But they were brothers and since their parents had died in a desperately cold winter eight years ago, they'd looked out for each other. Trying to persuade them to go along with his plan would probably result in a bitter argument that would do the one thing Jack had never expected to happen and break them up.

'Here's the situation,' he said, his tone serious enough to wipe the eager smiles from Emmet's and Horace's faces. 'We've stolen this gold. We know we shouldn't have. We know we're in a whole heap of trouble. We know both the groups we saw are now looking for the gold, and so us.'

Jack looked at each man, receiving sombre nods.

'And both groups saw us head to the wagon,' Emmet said.

'But,' Horace added, 'we were a long way away and they were ignoring us. I don't reckon they'd recognize us.'

'You're both right,' Jack said. 'So, the way I see it, we can do four things. We can leave the gold here. We can take the gold to the law. We can steal it. Or we can take a few bars and leave the rest.'

Jack rolled back on his haunches and he was pleased that both his brothers matched his action and thought before they responded. But the top of the box was open and the steady glow from inside was providing its own form of encouragement.

Horace responded first with the answer Jack had expected and feared.

'I say we take it all,' he said.

Emmet drew a sharp intake of breath. 'I say we take two — no three — bars apiece and leave the rest.'

Jack sighed. These responses didn't make his decision any easier. Long minutes passed as he stared at the lake below, and Emmet and Horace stayed quiet as he deliberated.

And, as he offered another silent wish that they'd never found the gold, a compromise came to him. It was sensible. It was cautious. It let them profit from their luck while keeping their options open to do the right thing later. And best of all, he reckoned Emmet would agree and Horace would accept it, after some grumbling.

'I reckon we close the box with *all* the gold still inside, then hide it somewhere where nobody will ever find it.'

A slow smile spread across Emmet's features, but Horace snorted.

'Hiding it ain't much use to us,' Horace muttered.

'Not yet it won't be,' Emmet said, nodding. 'But Jack is right. One day, say in five years when everyone's starting to forget about what happened, we can dig it up, and nobody will suspect us when we start spending the gold.'

'Five years is a long time to wait when we ain't got nothing now,' Horace grumbled. 'Can't we just take one bar?'

'Not even one bar,' Jack said.

Emmet patted Horace's arm. 'I ain't that pleased either, Horace, but Jack's plan is the right one. The likes of us turning up with gold bars right now will look mighty suspicious.'

'Yeah, but . . . ' Horace went on to list several good reasons why hiding the gold was a bad idea, but Jack let him have his say. It was his youngest brother's way of convincing himself that something was right and Jack knew he'd see the sense of this plan, eventually.

Emmet was also familiar with Horace's rants. He shuffled round to look into the box and started edging the bars apart to count them.

'Finished?' Jack said when Horace quietened.

Horace sighed, then jumped to his feet and kicked at the earth.

'Yeah. We hide the gold for now, like you said, but I ain't waiting no five years. I say we keep on listening out and when we reckon everyone's forgotten about it, we dig it up.'

Jack agreed to Horace's idea, which could either shorten or lengthen the time until they reclaimed the gold, and he glanced at Emmet to see if he agreed, but Emmet was peering into the box.

'You agree, too, Emmet?'

'Yeah, I agree we don't spend this gold for a while,' Emmet said, his voice abstracted. He reached into the box, then emerged with a fistful of bills. 'But nobody's going to tell me we can't spend this money right now.'

Horace whooped with delight and even Jack couldn't stop a huge grin breaking out as they hurried over to join Emmet.

'I thought there was just gold in there,' Horace said, peering into the box.

Emmet slapped the bills on the ground, then reached in and removed a second bundle.

'Nope. Right in the middle was this here money.'

'How much?'

Emmet peered into the box, confirming he'd extracted all the money, then flicked through the bills. He whistled under his breath.

'At least five hundred dollars.' He looked at Emmet's and Jack's smiling faces, then winked. 'Each.'

'Five hundred dollars each,' Horace exclaimed, swirling round to face Jack. 'Even if we're hiding the gold, we got to keep that, haven't we?'

Faced with his brothers' eager grins, Jack could only nod.

★   ★   ★

In Bluff Creek, Denver Calhoun pulled the wagon up outside Doc Swanson's house.

For the last six months Denver had made it his sole quest to round up the Flynn gang. There were six of them, each having a $1,000 bounty on his head with Flynn himself having a $5,000 bounty. $10,000 had been enough encouragement to attract every bounty hunter in the state, but none of them had got as close as Denver had.

He understood how the Flynn gang operated. Although the six men had raided numerous banks, they often used local lowlifes for individual raids, and these men were of limited ambition. And they were easier to catch than the elusive Flynn.

Denver hadn't fooled himself into believing the group he'd rounded up would be worth much, but more valuable was the possibility that they'd lead him to Flynn. And, as soon as he'd handed over the injured man to a doctor and the law, he planned to find the wounded man who had escaped.

The sight of a man riding into town with a wagonload of bullet-ridden bodies had attracted a trailing gaggle of people, who were not coming too close, but were ensuring they were close enough to watch developments.

To allay their concerns, Denver hailed the nearest person and told him to fetch Sheriff Mitchell. That man informed him that he wasn't in town, but he did scurry off to locate a deputy as Denver hauled the bound Rico Warren off the back of the wagon.

He hadn't checked on his prisoner since leaving the outlaws' hideout, but he had reckoned this man was resilient enough to have survived. And sure enough, he was still breathing. Blood stained his shirt, but it hadn't spread far enough to soak through to his jacket. Denver judged this a good sign and, with one hand on Rico's rope and the other clutching his gun, he led him into Swanson's house.

The doctor was an old friend and greeted him warmly, then led him through to his surgery where Denver pushed Rico into a chair.

'One of the Flynn gang?' Swanson asked, considering the injured man.

'Nope, but I'm getting closer. So, I'd be obliged if you'd help this one to live. I reckon he might have a story to tell.'

The hunched Rico shrugged away

from Doc Swanson's probing fingers, and even regained enough strength to jump up from his chair, but Denver pushed him back into it.

'Quit struggling,' Denver said, 'or you'll get a matching hole.'

Rico glared up at Denver, but then his eyes glazed and closed and his head slumped to lie on his chest. Denver helped Swanson remove the ropes from his wrists, then backed away a pace to stand by the wall.

'You can leave while I see what I can do,' Swanson said while he opened Rico's shirt-buttons. 'From the look of all this blood, he'll be out for a while.'

'I'll stay, in case he talks.'

'He won't be talking for quite a . . . ' Swanson snorted then gestured to Denver. 'Come look at this.'

Denver pushed himself from the wall and joined Swanson. He looked down at Rico's exposed chest and although he saw a small patch of dried blood, he couldn't see a bullet wound.

'Where did I hit him?'

Swanson drew Rico's shirt back over his chest, then poked a finger through the bullet hole, the finger emerging to stab into Rico's unblemished side.

'My guess is that this is someone else's shirt and he ain't been shot anywhere.'

Denver snorted then lunged down and grabbed Rico's collar. He dragged him up from the chair.

'Is that right?' he snapped.

Rico stayed slumped in his grip a moment, but then opened an eye and provided a wide grin.

'Guess I might not have been as injured as I made out,' he said with humour in his tone.

Doc Swanson sighed as he turned away. 'And I reckon I can hear Deputy Fairborn coming in. I'll leave you to deal with this one.'

As the front door opened and Doc Swanson headed into the corridor, calling out to the deputy to come to the surgery, Denver gained a firmer grip of Rico's collar and pulled him up on tiptoe.

'What kind of damn fool trick was that?'

'Didn't want to die,' Rico said, smiling. 'And I thought I might get a chance to run.'

'Then you're stupid as well as conniving.' Denver opened his grip, letting Rico regain his footing. 'But it did you no good. I'm handing you over to the law now.'

'Don't,' Rico said as Deputy Fairborn paced down the corridor with Doc Swanson muttering at his side. 'Hand me over to the law and I'll say nothing. Keep me out of a cell and I'll tell you how to find Flynn and claim the biggest bounty any man could ever want.'

As Denver glared at Rico, Deputy Fairborn headed into the surgery.

'You sure rounded up plenty of trouble out there, Denver,' he said.

'Sure did,' Denver said, still looking into Rico's wide-open and pleading eyes.

'That another one of Flynn's gang?'

Rico raised his eyebrows.

'Nope.' Denver slapped a hand on Rico's shoulder and gripped it tightly as he swung him round to face the deputy. 'This here is my partner.'

3

'What you planning on doing?' Jack Turner asked as he headed out of the livery stables in Bluff Creek.

'Getting a bath, a shave, some decent clothes on me and some decent food inside me,' Emmet said, 'then getting me the drunkest I've ever been.'

'I'm finding a poker-game,' Horace said, 'and then I'm finding the liveliest saloon-girl in town and showing her what two months spent with only you two for company does to a man.'

Emmet laughed. 'What about you, Jack?'

Jack rubbed his bearded chin while considering. He'd not approved of the decision to head into town, reckoning that staying away from other people for as long as possible was the most sensible policy. But with the gold buried, his brothers had outvoted him.

Now, standing in the middle of a bustling town with more money than he'd ever owned pressing against his chest, his former grumpy mood evaporated.

'Reckon as I might do all of them,' he said.

As Horace joined Emmet in laughing, Emmet glanced around.

'We staying together tonight?' he asked.

'Ain't looking for no argument,' Horace said, 'but as I said, after two months spent with you two, I ain't doing that.'

Emmet and Jack grunted their agreement and, after promising to meet up the next day, Horace and Emmet turned to head away, but Jack called them back.

'Just remember what I said,' he cautioned. 'Three brothers all flush with money will look mighty odd, so don't go drawing attention to yourselves and don't give nobody no cause to think you've found a whole heap of money. Keep your billfolds well-hidden and don't go too wild. We can have plenty more nights like tonight if we're sensible.'

Emmet and Horace looked at each other, wicked grins spreading across both their faces, then turned back to Jack.

'You can trust me, Jack,' Emmet said.

'Yeah,' Horace said, smirking. 'I'll stay well out of trouble.'

And, with those promises made, they slapped each other on the back then swung round to head off into the heaving and raucous Bluff Creek, leaving Jack standing on the boardwalk.

A twinge of anxiety hit him as his brothers disappeared from view, but then his gaze roved round to centre on the bath-house and, with a rub of his hands, he headed across the road.

★   ★   ★

'I don't bluff,' Denver Calhoun said, leaning back in his chair.

38

The young trapper to Denver's right peered at Denver over his cards and gave a confident smile.

'So you've said, but this time, I'll pay the ten dollars to find out.' He peeled a bill from the pile before him and skimmed it into the centre of the table.

Denver had been minded to head out of Bluff Creek and take his new, and untrustworthy, partner's advice as to where Flynn was hiding out. But when Deputy Fairborn had reported that several men from Stonewall had ridden through town earlier and had asked for him, he decided to wait awhile.

Stonewall was a forgotten excuse for a town, which attracted men who enjoyed trouble. So, he figured that staying in town would let whatever trouble those men represented move on, and he could let Rico sweat a while longer over what the result of any more duplicity would be.

Denver glanced at his cards, then ran his gaze across the other poker-players as he prolonged the moment before he laid down his hand.

Doc Swanson had dropped out of the hand. He'd been sullen all evening, being uncomfortable with Denver's decision to keep Rico out of jail, but going along with it because he trusted Denver. Rico had backed out as soon as he could and sat with his hands on his lap and his head lowered. The Texan banker was watching the trapper's reactions with interest.

But, over the trapper's shoulder, Denver saw two men wander into the saloon and peer around.

Both men were stocky and trail-dirty. Their surly glares suggested to Denver that whoever they were looking for would face trouble.

'Come on, Denver,' the trapper said. 'I just got to know if you got yourself a flush.'

Denver firmed his jaw. He glanced at each of his fellow-players, but still kept a part of his attention on the newcomers.

But then the taller man's gaze

centred on the poker-game beside the bar and, with a slap of his hand against the other man's chest, he rolled his shoulders and strode across the saloon.

With his gaze set on Denver, he swung to a halt behind the trapper.

'You be Denver Calhoun?' he asked.

'Yep,' Denver said. He fingered his cards, then shuffled one card from the centre to the outside. 'What you want?'

'Be obliged if you'd come outside.'

'Why?'

'Just come with us.' The man wiped his mouth with the back of a shaking hand. 'We got to . . . We got to take you somewhere.'

Denver fanned his cards out, nodding to himself, then closed them into a pile and laid them on the table, face down.

'Hey,' the trapper said, 'you can show me what you got before you — '

With a cold flash of his eyes, Denver silenced him, then looked up and peered from one man to the other.

Both men were twitchy. They were

trying to appear arrogant but, from the way they glanced at each other, Denver reckoned they'd dreaded this confrontation.

'Well, like my good friend here says, you boys will have to wait. I'm in a right friendly game of poker and my friend can't wait for me to take his money.' Denver smiled as the trapper snorted. 'So, unless you tell me what you want, I'm staying.'

'We just . . . ' the man squeaked. He coughed to clear his throat, then restarted in a deeper voice. 'We just want you to come with us and see something outside.'

The second man grunted and pushed his colleague aside to stand before the table with his hands on his hips.

'What he's trying to say,' he muttered, 'is that you're coming with us whether you want to or not.'

This time the trapper and the banker gathered the gist of the menace these men represented and scraped back their chairs from the table. The morose Rico stayed hunched, but when Doc Swanson slapped him in the chest, he sat bolt upright, then rolled out his chair and ran for the bar, leaving only Denver sitting opposite the newcomers.

'Why?'

'You killed a man in Stonewall.'

'Never been there.'

'He came into the saloon all shot up. Before he died, he said you killed him.'

Denver rolled his gaze from one man to the other, receiving a nervous glance from the first man and a wide-eyed glare from the second. Stonewall was closer to the house where he'd captured Rico Warren than Bluff Creek, so the dead man could be the escaped outlaw.

He gripped the edge of the table, then shuffled forward, the action masking his right hand slipping to his holster before he laid both hands on his lap.

'This dead man a friend of yours?'

'Yeah.' The man pointed at Denver. 'And put those hands where I can see them or *you* won't live long enough to leave this saloon.'

'And if *you* don't leave right now, you'll die where you stand.'

Denver stared at the man but kept his hands beneath the table. He sat like a statue, the long moment dragging a bead of sweat from the man's brow.

The man exchanged a glance with his colleague. An unspoken message passed between them as they raised their eyebrows.

Then they whirled their hands to their holsters, but Denver had already slipped his Peacemaker from its holster and blasted hot lead up through the table. The slug tore into the first man's neck, spinning him back and to the floor.

With his other hand Denver knocked the table up, slamming it into the other man's chest and forcing his gun arm up.

A redirected shot whistled over Denver's head, but before the man had extricated himself from the furniture, Denver had already stood and ripped a slug through the wood and into the man's chest.

The man stumbled back a pace, the table falling away from him, but a second slug wheeled him into the bar for him to lie sprawled over the counter.

For a moment Denver stood, one hand raised and poised, his gun thrust out, until sure that these men didn't have any accomplices elsewhere in the saloon; then he twirled the gun back into its holster.

As his fellow poker-players righted the table, Denver collected his spilt cards, then threw them on the table, face up, displaying his flush.

'Like I promised,' Denver said, looking at the trapper. 'I never bluff.'

★　★　★

'Now,' Jack Turner said, 'what's a right pretty young thing like you called?'

'For you I'll answer to Sally,' the saloon-girl said, accompanying her flirting with a fluttering of eyelashes.

45

'And what's a fancy-dressed man like you called?'

'I'm Jack Turner.' Jack straightened the cuffs of his crisp new jacket and leaned on the bar. 'But you can call me anything you like.'

Sally leaned towards him, sniffing, her gaze darting up and down his body and her eager smile suggesting that Jack's gleaming skin, freshly shaved chin, and lacquered hair was meeting with her approval.

'You want me to think up a name right now?' She glanced at the stairs with a darting twitch of her eyes. 'Or do you want me to do that thinking later?'

Jack was minded to let her lead him upstairs now, but he also fancied getting a whiskey or two inside him first. So he ordered drinks for them both, then settled down to enjoy talking with someone a whole heap more appealing than Horace or Emmet.

But before he'd finished half his drink or even managed another flirting exchange, he was already regretting not taking Sally up on her initial offer. Emmet came blustering into the saloon, red of face and the napkin tucked into his collar suggesting a frantic change of plans.

'Whatever trouble Horace is in can wait,' Jack said when Emmet joined him, not waiting for his brother to explain himself as he kept his admiring gaze on Sally's appealing oval face. 'I'm talking with a right pretty young woman and she's the only important thing in my life right now.'

'But you got to come,' Emmet demanded. 'He's in a poker-game.'

Jack winked at Sally, received an encouraging giggle, then swung round to lean back against the bar. He laid a hand on Emmet's shoulder.

'Horace is a better player than either you or me.' Jack dug his fingers into Emmet's shoulder, then pushed him back a pace. 'Go away.'

Emmet leaned forward. 'The other players are this bounty hunter, this Texan banker and — '

Jack slapped a hand over Emmet's mouth. He kept the hand there while glaring into his eyes, silently conveying with his firm jaw and narrowed eyes that he didn't want to hear any more, then released him and swung round to face Sally.

But she'd already gathered the gist of the direction this conversation was taking and was now fawning over another man.

'Like I said,' Jack grunted, pushing Emmet away and shuffling back into Sally's eye-line. 'Horace will be fine, if a bit poorer.'

Emmet muscled in beside Jack and swung him round to face the door.

'But the bounty hunter's already killed two men, and they weren't even playing.'

Jack winced, but as Sally was ignoring him and flirting with the better prospect, he raised his glass to his lips.

'Perhaps I will check on him, but after I've enjoyed a few more drinks.'

'You ain't got the time. The stakes

have just gone no-limit.'

Jack slammed the glass back on the counter, tipped his hat to the distracted Sally, then tore the napkin from Emmet's collar. They hurried outside. On the way to the Lucky Star saloon Emmet related the story as he'd heard it. And none of it made good listening.

Horace had joined a poker-game. It had started in a friendly enough way. But then two men had ridden into town looking to pick a fight with the bounty hunter over a dead man in Stonewall, and they'd paid with hot lead. That had generated plenty of interest in the poker-game and, with a crowd watching the players' every move, Horace had forgotten Jack's final instructions and raised the stakes.

At first his foolhardy behaviour had worked. Within a few hands, Horace had taken fifty dollars off the Texan banker. With grim determination the banker played on, but his losses mounted. Then came one hand where the banker wouldn't back down and, with the other players throwing in their cards, Horace had locked horns with him.

The banker's offer to make the stakes no-limit and Horace's acceptance had generated a wave of anticipation that had spread to Ma Johnson's eatery where Emmet was enjoying his third helping of apple-pie.

And when Jack and Emmet headed into the Lucky Star saloon, a solid wall of people had spread out around the poker-table, with people standing on chairs, tables and lining the stairs to watch the game.

They barged their way into claiming a table to stand on where they could look down on the game.

Jack saw that Horace was facing him and sporting a huge grin. He'd acquired a cigar, and whiskey glasses littered the table. He was rubbing his chin, glancing around and grinning as he enjoyed being the centre of attention in a high-stakes poker-game, when he usually got over-excited if the pot hit a dollar.

'I'll match that,' Horace said, then glanced around the mass of watching people. His roving gaze caught Jack and Emmet and he favoured them with a toothy grin before moving on. 'And I'll raise you two hundred.'

'You reckon you can afford that?' the banker said.

'I'd hoped you'd ask.' Horace extracted a wad from his pocket and counted out bills until a pile was in the centre of the table. 'Two hundred dollars in cash, or is that too high for you?'

Muttering drifted around the watching customers, but over on the table at the front of the saloon, Jack and Emmet exchanged shakes of their heads.

'So much for not drawing attention to ourselves,' Jack said.

Emmet shrugged. 'We ain't had money before. You can't blame him for going loco.'

'Suppose I can't, try as I might.'

Jack returned to watching the game.

'You know the stakes are no-limit,' the banker said, 'don't you?'

'I ain't no idiot,' Horace said. He paused to take a puff of the cigar, then gulped to avoid coughing. 'I've raised your bet, in cash.'

'You have, but what are you going to do if I raise again?'

Horace closed his eyes a moment as the banker reached into his pocket and withdrew an even larger wad than Horace had produced. He hurled it into the centre of the table, without counting, the bills fanning out.

'It'll cost you five hundred to stay in the game.'

Horace lowered his head. He gathered the bills he'd won earlier into a pile and counted through them, but Jack could tell he was going to fall well short.

Horace sighed, then looked up, catching Jack's eye. Jack returned a shake of the head, then a nod towards the door, but Emmet gave an eager nod, then jumped down from the table.

Jack flinched then dropped to his knees to slap a hand on Emmet's shoulder, halting him.

'Where you going?' he asked.

Emmet pointed. 'To get in on the game.'

'Leave it. Horace's gone way over his head with this one.'

'He ain't, not any more. We're wealthy men now.' Emmet grinned at Jack and when Jack continued to frown, he shrugged. 'Come on. It'll be fun.'

Emmet shrugged away from Jack's grip then wended a path through the throng.

Jack watched him go while shaking his head, then sighed and jumped down from the table to follow. They emerged from the crowd to stand beside the poker-table, Horace welcoming them in, and they stood in a huddle, whispering.

Jack didn't bother trying to persuade Horace and Emmet to back off, as Horace was already in too deep to listen to sense. And as the money in his pocket wasn't his either, he didn't check what Horace's hand was and followed Emmet's lead in giving Horace everything he had.

Horace didn't even count the money as he collected the bills into a large pile, then stood over the banker and slammed them down on the table.

'There,' he said, 'I haven't even counted it either, but there's plenty more where that came from. And I reckon I'm still in the game.'

'Seems you are,' the banker said, eyeing the huge pile of cash.

Horace shuffled the bills apart. 'And I reckon it'll cost you plenty to match that, unless you hadn't realized the stakes are no-limit.'

'The stakes *are* no-limit, and as I'd never be so foolish as to carry that amount of cash around with me, you'll have to accept this.' The banker reached into his pocket, withdrew an envelope, and wrote out an IOU. He signed it, then glanced over his shoulder. A man slipped out of the crowd and glanced at the envelope, then counter-signed.

'I want to see cash,' Horace said,

blinking rapidly, 'not some piece of paper.'

'What you're seeing here is better than cash. It's my signature and another businessman's signature on a piece of paper that is a testament to my credentials as an honourable man.' The banker pushed the envelope into the centre of the table. 'I raise you two thousand dollars.'

As Jack and Emmet glanced at each other and shook their heads, Horace gulped.

'Still want to see cash,' he grumbled. 'How do I know you'll pay up when you lose?'

'*If* I lose,' the banker grunted, then rocked forward to glare at Horace over the table. 'And do not question my integrity again. I am a successful man and I can easily afford to cover that bet.'

Horace nodded as he met the banker's gaze.

'Easily afford, you say?'

The banker settled back into his chair, took a puff on his cigar, then raised his chin to expel a torrent of smoke high into the air.

'I can, but that's not important now. The only thing that matters is whether you can match my bet.' He looked Horace up and down. 'Or is the bet too high for you? Perhaps you'd prefer to throw in your cards.'

'I ain't throwing these in. I can match your bet.'

'You forget. Everyone knows me and my reputation. I can get twenty signatures to testify that I can honour my debts. You got anyone who can vouch for you?'

'Don't need nobody to do that. I can show you right here.' Horace reached into his pocket, rummaged around, then whipped out his hand, a flash of gold blurring. 'I bet one gold bar.'

Horace slammed the bar down in the centre of the table atop the bills. The draught fluttered several bills to the floor.

Standing beside the table in full view of over one hundred people, Jack and Emmet looked at each other and winced.

4

'What you got?' Deputy Fairborn asked.

The undertaker turned away from the two bodies on the table to look at Denver Calhoun then at Fairborn.

'This might be better,' he whispered, 'if I talk to you on our own.'

'I trust Denver. I keep no secrets from him. If you got information, he can hear it.'

Denver grunted his agreement as the undertaker shrugged and then removed a sheet of folded paper from the body on the left's jacket. A neat bullet hole and accompanying bloodstain marred the paper.

'They both carried one of these.'

Denver considered the undertaker's raised eyebrows, but when no more information was forthcoming, he took the paper and flicked it open.

It was a wanted poster. The crime

was the murder of an unnamed man. The wanted man was Denver Calhoun. And Sheriff Mitchell was offering a bounty of one gold bar on Denver's head.

After telling the undertaker to keep this news to himself, Fairborn and Denver headed outside.

'Your boss often raise bounties on innocent men?' Denver asked.

Fairborn stopped on the boardwalk and looked up and down the road.

'He's a fair man in my experience. I guess he has his reasons.'

'Either way, I'm obliged to you for not taking that bounty offer seriously.'

'But I do.' Fairborn stared at Denver, his firm gaze letting him know that his decision could change; then he patted Denver's shoulder and headed across the road towards the Lucky Star saloon. 'You got any idea who the murdered man was?'

'One of those outlaws escaped when I shot them up and he could have headed to Stonewall. But what's more

interesting is the bounty. Ain't ever heard of anyone offering a gold . . . '
Denver rubbed his forehead and stopped to look aloft.

Fairborn stopped and considered Denver.

'What you just thought of?'

'When I shot that man in the hideout, he had a gold bar on him. Just surmising, but perhaps that's become the bounty on me.'

'Why would Mitchell do that?' Fairborn mused.

Denver shrugged, considering but failing to think of a reason. But then he noticed that the Lucky Star saloon was crowded beyond capacity and that the Golden Horn saloon across the road was deserted. When Fairborn had asked him to come with him, the poker-game had been attracting attention, but nothing like this.

With Fairborn at his side, he set off towards the crowded saloon.

'Like I said, I'm just surmising. You got any idea where the gold could have come from?'

'Nope. Haven't heard of any gold going missing recently. You?'

Denver shook his head as they halted at the back of the throng of people outside the saloon. In the tightly packed room people were standing on chairs and tables and milling outside at the door and windows, craning their necks while on tiptoe as they tried to see inside.

The two men glanced at each other then barged their way in.

The crowd pushed back, everyone eager to keep their position, but then moved aside as they saw that Deputy Fairborn was trying to get past them. Denver chose his own route and, as he used the simpler tactic of kicking or shoving people aside, he was several paces ahead of the lawman when the trouble broke out.

Dollars, exposed cards and a gold bar lay on the poker-table that was attracting the attention, but the banker was standing and confronting Horace, the trapper who had insisted on raising the stakes before Denver had left the game.

The banker stood crouched with his back to Denver. The people standing between Denver and the table stopped him from having a complete view of what he was doing, although the sudden surge of people peeling away behind Horace suggested he'd drawn a gun.

Horace raised his hands, shaking his head, but a gunshot ripped out wheeling him away.

Everyone dived for cover as Horace hit the floor, his chest holed, but two other men who were standing by the table didn't duck. These men scrambled for their guns, but the banker had the hair-trigger reflexes of all card-sharks. He turned at the hip, his gun arcing round, but before he could fire, Denver emptied a slug into his back, sprawling him into the table.

The banker clawed himself to a standing position, but his gun fell from his slack fingers and he tumbled to the floor.

And then Fairborn wrestled himself clear of the sprawl of people and stood over the shot banker. He demanded that the two men the banker had turned on throw down their guns. Then he set about questioning everyone, and the customers were eager to provide a summary of what had happened.

Denver relaxed when he heard confirmation of his theory that the banker had cheated, then started the gunfight. And when Fairborn took the dead man's colleagues away for further questioning, he accompanied them to the jailhouse. Once inside, Denver leaned back against the wall as Fairborn questioned them through the bars.

Although Fairborn treated the men as if they were outlaws, Denver rapidly saw that this wasn't the case. Both men were young and had the wild-eyed and scared look of men who had got themselves caught up in a dangerous situation that was beyond their experience.

But they were also nervous enough to

make it clear they were hiding something. And as both men were wearing baggy new clothes, the information they were hiding was probably to do with how they'd obtained money and a gold bar recently.

Denver grew bored with listening to the lies the men were spinning, and turned his thoughts to how he'd track down Flynn. Rico was an unreliable source of information, but if the outlaw he'd shot had died in Stonewall, he was his only source of information, so when Fairborn relented from his questioning and left the jailhouse, Denver followed him.

As Denver had requested earlier, Rico was mounted up and ready to move on out, but Denver and Fairborn stood on the boardwalk facing each other.

'One gold bar turning up is bizarre,' Denver said. 'Two ain't.'

'Agreed,' Fairborn said, nodding, 'but I still got no idea where they're coming from.'

'Then question those men some more.'

'I will, but even when they provide an answer, I don't reckon they're the kind of men who'll have stolen a gold bar. I reckon they got themselves some luck.'

'Yeah, bad luck.' Denver tipped his hat to Fairborn, then turned to his horse, but Fairborn raised a hand, halting him.

'Just note, Denver, that there's something going on here and I trust you enough to believe you're not behind it. So, you can leave, but . . . '

Fairborn raised his eyebrows, inviting a response.

'I understand and I'm obliged to you for not arresting me. But if Mitchell makes things difficult for you, I will hand myself in until you can sort things out.'

'I'm not worried about Mitchell. I'm letting you go because I reckon you can get to the bottom of this when you ain't wasting your time in a cell facing nonsense charges.'

Denver sighed. 'Then I got to be honest with you. I ain't interested in this gold. I'm going after the bounty on Flynn.'

'I know, but I reckon the gold and Flynn have to be connected in a way neither of us can see right now.'

Fairborn bade Denver goodbye, then turned away, leaving Denver to mount up and nudge his horse round to stand beside Rico. Denver glanced at his partner from the corner of his eye.

'You've impressed me, *partner*,' he said. 'You followed my orders.'

'I have,' Rico said, watching Fairborn head back into the jailhouse. 'And when are we moving out?'

Denver followed Rico's gaze to look at the jailhouse.

'As soon as you've had a good long look at the jailhouse because, unless you want to see it from the inside, you'll lead me to Flynn without any tricks or lies or distractions.'

Rico nodded then pointed ahead. 'In that case, we go that-a-way.'

Denver glared at Rico a moment longer then moved on out.

★ ★ ★

Jack Turner leaned back against the bars to his cell. In the adjoining cell Emmet was lying on his bunk, but from his quiet breathing Jack could tell he wasn't sleeping.

'You reckon the deputy will question us again?' Jack asked, his voice low.

'Don't reckon as he will,' Emmet murmured. 'He can't think we're guilty of anything or he wouldn't have kept us in the cells next to each other where we can talk.'

Jack snorted. 'I reckon he knows we'll do that. He kept us together so we can talk ourselves into getting real worried.'

'That won't work. I'm already real worried.'

Jack grunted his agreement and rolled round to lie on his bunk. With grim determination he tried to sleep while fighting down the fears that had threatened to overwhelm ever since he'd let Emmet and Horace talk him into stealing the gold.

But sleep proved elusive and first light was slotting in through the bars of the cell's window when he finally grabbed a few hours of troubling and unrestful sleep.

And his worries didn't recede as the next day wore on.

Periodically, Deputy Fairborn called into the jailhouse, but he didn't look at them, and curiously, his failure to question them worried Jack more effectively than intense questioning would have done.

Throughout the day Jack avoided talking with Emmet, figuring that after their brother's death nothing they could say to each other would cheer the other person up.

Evening was approaching when Deputy Fairborn came to their cells and, without looking at either man, unlocked the doors then stood back.

'That mean you've proved we're

innocent?' Emmet said, jumping to his feet and hurrying through the open door.

'It don't work like that,' Fairborn said. He headed to his desk and removed their guns, then their money. 'I reckon you're guilty of plenty, but as I've no idea what it is, I got no choice but to let you go and give you back your money.'

Jack followed Emmet across the room to stand before the desk. He lowered his head with a suitable level of contriteness, but Emmet snorted.

'Our brother had some property,' he said. 'You know he didn't cheat in that poker-game so we ought to get his gold and — '

Jack elbowed Emmet in the stomach, silencing him, then darted him a harsh glare that told him not to question their luck. But, as Emmet had complained, Fairborn berated both men with a lengthy and stern warning about what would happen if they ever brought themselves to his attention again. Then he pushed them outside on to the boardwalk.

Both men shuffled away and across the road to the livery stables.

'What we doing now?' Emmet asked.

Jack sighed. 'Reckon as we find out what happened to Horace's body and give him a decent burial.'

'And then what?'

'You heard the deputy. We're men under suspicion of doing something. We're only out of those cells because he don't know what it is.'

'Don't understand that. Somebody . . . ' Emmet glanced around, confirming that nobody was close enough to hear him. 'Somebody must be annoyed that their gold's gone missing. You'd have thought he'd make the connection and keep us locked up.'

'Then that must mean nobody's reported it missing yet, but as soon as word gets out, that lawman won't take long to figure out we had something to do with it and come looking for us.'

Emmet stopped to kick at the dirt in

the centre of the road.

'I was afraid you were going to say that. We ain't going to be able to touch that gold for years and years and years.'

'And we both got to start acting a whole heap more sensibly than we did last night.'

Emmet kicked away one last huge swipe of dirt, then gave a slow nod.

'That mean we got to put some distance between us and that gold?'

'You got the right idea.' Jack looked down the road in the general direction of Broken Rock Canyon, then over his shoulder. 'Reckon as we should head to Stonewall first. That place's got to be safer than here.'

5

The cave below was quiet and didn't appear occupied, but Denver Calhoun was taking no chances and was keeping watch until he was certain.

Beside him, Rico was growing increasingly restless, but as Denver didn't trust anything his untrustworthy and temporary partner told him, he was ignoring his mood.

He hadn't expected Rico to be immediately forthcoming on how he could find Flynn, and had expected he'd need plenty of encouragement to get any clues out of him. But after they'd spent the night in a short blind canyon thirty miles out of Bluff Creek, Rico had directed him to this remote spot at the far end of Broken Rock Canyon without any detours.

As the sun edged towards the mountains Denver decided it was safe to investigate and, with Rico scurrying along beside him, he headed to the cave, taking the most careful and stealthy approach possible.

After almost an hour of steadily running from covering boulder to covering boulder, he pressed his back to the wall beside the cave. He counted to ten, then darted a glance inside.

The cave was larger than it appeared from the outside, stretching back for fifty yards. The low sun let him see into all corners; they were deserted.

He darted back, then grabbed Rico's arm and pushed him into the cave ahead of him. When Rico had shuffled several paces in to the cave without any unexpected noises sounding, he followed him.

He noted the signs of human habitation — a sprawl of festering blankets, a mouldering animal carcass, but that didn't stop him from tapping a foot on the ground as he waited for Rico to turn around.

'Well,' he said, when Rico's roving

gaze had taken in the cave, 'where is he?'

'I don't know,' Rico whined, 'I just don't. This is where I reckoned he'd be hiding out.'

'You only reckon? And it don't mean you lied to me?'

Rico gulped. 'I wouldn't do that. You got to believe me.'

'Believing you is the last thing I'll ever do. I want some answers now or I'm taking you back to that jailhouse.'

Rico swirled round on the spot, looking around the cave, then nodded. 'Maybe I got me an idea. Flynn was supposed to be here by now, but he ain't, so something must have delayed him.'

'And where does that mean he is?'

Rico pointed out through the cave entrance.

'Somewhere along Broken Rock Canyon.'

'Heading that way takes us closer to Bluff Creek and a certain jailhouse.' Denver clamped a hand on Rico's shoulder and dragged him outside. 'You'd better hope we find him. I'm out of patience with you.'

That warning had the desired effect, and within the hour Rico located a rarely used trail that Denver didn't know about which took them down into Broken Rock Canyon. As night was closing they camped out for a second night beside the snaking river at the bottom.

Denver made no special arrangements to guard Rico, judging that his instincts were sharp enough to stop him if he tried to escape or attack him.

For his part Rico remained quiet. When he did speak it was only to reply to questions with sharp retorts. But whether his sullen attitude resulted from his worrying about an impeding encounter with Flynn or the possibility of Denver taking him back to jail, Denver couldn't tell.

At first light they set off, following the winding river which gradually widened as they headed down the canyon.

Rico provided no clues as to where Flynn might be along the canyon and Denver resisted the temptation to encourage him to talk, deciding that his initial threat should suffice.

The morning wore on with no sign of Flynn, and Rico made no claims that they were getting closer, but Denver noticed that Rico was spending an increasing amount of time glancing around. His demeanour suggested that he expected to see someone at the top of the canyon or perhaps beyond the next bend.

Denver kept this observation to himself, figuring that he didn't want to alert Rico to the fact that he knew an ambush might be about to happen.

But when the canyon deepened and widened so that the top was 800 feet above them and he could see for miles ahead, Denver judged the likelihood of Flynn's having a secure location from which to ambush him as remote. He drew his horse alongside Rico's.

'You ain't convincing me you know

where Flynn is,' Denver said. 'Tell me something now that'll stop me taking you back to jail.'

'I can only tell you the truth,' Rico said. 'That was my house you raided. I let Flynn use it as a safe place. I don't ask no questions and that's the way Flynn likes it.'

'That don't exactly make you innocent.'

'It don't, but it don't exactly make me guilty of much either.'

'And what was Flynn doing when he last used your hideout?'

'Like I said, I don't ask no questions.'

'But it had something to do with a gold bar?'

Rico firmed his jaw, shaking his head.

'I'll take you to Flynn,' he said, 'but I'm not answering that.'

Denver nodded, feeling a hint of respect for Rico. His opinion of this man had veered from at best his being someone who would sell out his own kin to save himself, to at worst being someone who was leading him into a trap. But perhaps he was neither and was actually treading a difficult path between satisfying Denver, Flynn, and himself.

'Then more than one gold bar?' Denver persisted, but Rico snorted his unwillingness to answer. 'More than the two that have turned up so far?'

'Don't waste your breath,' Rico snapped. 'I won't talk about no gold.'

'You won't talk, but that lets me know there is something for you to not talk about.' Denver watched Rico sneer. 'And even if you won't answer my questions, Flynn won't like it when he finds out you've double-crossed him.'

'I haven't double-crossed him. I'm keeping myself out of jail and leading you to your death.' Rico laughed. 'Flynn will fill you so full of bullets, you'll rattle.'

Denver judged Rico's comment as being the most honest he'd heard so far, and he searched for more ways to probe him and perhaps get him to inadvertently reveal information.

But then those thoughts fled when he saw the land beyond the next bend in the canyon opening up to him. It was still around a mile away, but beyond, buzzards were circling.

Rico noticed Denver's interest and turned round in the saddle. He flinched, his reaction dragging a grim smile out of Denver.

'Maybe,' Denver said, 'Flynn is the one who's full of holes.'

* * *

Despite the urgency of moving on Jack and Emmet still wanted to take Horace back to their house in the mountains and bury him beside their parents. But they had to agree that when they'd stolen the gold they'd lost the chance of providing him with such a dignified resting place.

So, on a bleak and windswept hill outside town, they buried him in a grave marked only by a simple scrawled epitaph beneath a stone. They stayed long enough to murmur their goodbyes.

Then they rode out of town, heading to Stonewall, both men remaining quiet and morose on the journey. In the little they did say, they agreed that they no longer entertained thoughts of spending their remaining windfall on wild fun.

In a strange way, Jack was more comfortable with his sombre mood. To sit on the knowledge of the location of the gold for years was always going to require fortitude. And the unfortunate results of their wild spree had reduced his enthusiasm for being rich and so made it easier for him to avoid going back for the gold.

In fact, Emmet confirmed that he now shared Jack's opinion that their lives would have been happier if they had never found the gold.

As the sun closed on the horizon the two downbeat brothers rode into Stonewall. A chill wind accompanied them, rustling dust down the town's only road.

Stonewall was smaller than Bluff

Creek and nowhere near as bustling. Only a few men were going about their business and they scurried to their destinations with their collars thrust high while showing no interest in the new arrivals.

Whereas Bluff Creek presented plenty of choice to its visitors, Stonewall had just one example of each of the basic amenities. So, after hitching their horses outside the only saloon, both men agreed that they saw no reason to stay here beyond the one night before they headed further east.

They ate a basic meal in a room beside the saloon, making sure that they counted out the exact change as if they hated spending their limited funds. Then they headed to the saloon to quietly drink away the evening in a sombre salute to their departed brother.

But on the wall outside the saloon a wanted poster caught Jack's eye. It had a good likeness of the bounty hunter who had killed the banker, but that didn't surprise Jack as much as the fact that the bounty on offer was one gold bar.

Emmet and Jack glanced at each other and winced.

'One gold bar,' Emmet murmured. 'I just don't believe it.'

'And Denver Calhoun is a wanted man. What's happening here?'

'Don't know, but I reckon we shouldn't stay to find out.'

Jack nodded and turned, but found that a portly man sporting a gap-toothed grin was looking at the poster over their shoulders. He had to flinch back a pace to avoid walking into him. Jack tipped his hat then moved to slip by, but the man held his arms wide and gathered Jack and Emmet up. He walked them closer to the poster.

'Sure find it hard to believe this poster, too,' he said with an arm draped over each man's shoulders. 'One gold bar.'

Jack glanced at the poster. 'Yeah, that's a mighty tempting bounty.'

'It sure is, but you ain't the first to be

tempted. Half the men in town are after Denver Calhoun, and I reckon anyone going after him needs a real advantage.' He slapped both men's shoulders then released them to point at his chest. 'And I reckon that Temple Kelly might have found one.'

'Then I wish you luck.' Jack moved to leave again, but Temple paced to the side and blocked his route.

'You didn't listen to what I'm saying.' He grinned. 'I reckon you two men are that advantage.'

'Then you thought wrong,' Jack said, looking at Emmet, who was already nervously biting his fingernails. 'We aren't going after Denver. We got business elsewhere.'

'And there was me thinking you knew how to track down Denver and that you'd share that information over a drink.' Temple patted his holster. 'Three men are better than two when going after someone like Denver Calhoun and a gold bar split three ways is better than no gold bar.'

'You're mistaken.' Jack hunched his shoulders, trying to look small and unthreatening. 'We aren't bounty hunters.'

'And neither am I. You see, I didn't rush off after Denver like the others. I asked around, gathering clues as to where he'd go. And I heard that he'd killed the first two men who found him, and that he'd killed another man who had a gold bar over a poker-table.'

'I hadn't heard that,' Jack said, trying to put as much conviction into his voice as possible.

'I'm surprised. It happened in Bluff Creek, and you rode into town from that direction.' Temple raised his eyebrows. 'And I heard that two men got arrested when Denver killed the man with the gold bar. And those men had a whole heap of money on them and were smartly dressed — just like you two.'

Jack firmed his jaw. 'Don't know about that. We've never been to Bluff Creek.'

'Perhaps I'm wrong, then.' Temple rocked from foot to foot, then turned away. 'But I reckon I'll check it out with Sheriff Mitchell. He's mighty interested in hearing any information about where those gold bars are coming from.'

'Don't do that,' Jack said, raising his voice and halting Temple. He sighed. 'Perhaps you'd prefer to have a drink with us instead.'

Temple swung round, grinning. 'I thought you might change your mind. I reckon we three are about to become a mighty fine team.'

He slapped both hands on Jack's and Emmet's backs, then ushered them into the saloon. At the bar he bought them whiskeys, then invited them to share the information they'd acquired.

Emmet had the sense to stay quiet and so let Jack provide only one version of events, but that left Jack little time to work out how much he could safely relate.

So, as Temple already knew about the poker-game, the gold, and the cash, he kept to the story he'd told Deputy Fairborn yesterday: they'd found some cash on the trail and didn't worry about where it had come from. They'd divided it up, but Horace had taken them both by surprise when he'd produced the gold bar.

Then he told a lengthy and honest tale about the poker-game, putting Temple right about the circumstances and stating that Denver hadn't killed Horace, but had acted to save them. He told him about their arrest and left the most interesting piece of information until the end when he reported that Denver had headed out of town, riding west towards the place where they'd found the money.

Temple listened to his tale with much nodding, giving the impression of a man who had spent plenty of time asking questions and hearing various versions of stories. Accordingly, he rechecked the details, taking any minor deviation as an excuse to pump Jack for more information. And to loosen Jack's tongue he refreshed his glass frequently, but Jack kept to his tale.

At last Temple declared himself contented.

'A mighty fine tale,' he said. 'And I reckon we got enough there for us to search for Denver.'

Jack fingered his whiskey-glass, pondering how best to get away from Temple without appearing suspicious, but Emmet intervened.

'You ain't been listening to Jack,' he said. 'We ain't going after Denver. He may have a bounty on his head, but he saved our lives and that's good enough for us to leave him alone. If you want to go after him, do that, but you can leave us out of it.'

Jack backed his brother up with a vigorous nod, then downed his whiskey and slammed the glass on the bar.

'I agree,' he said. 'You got the information you wanted. Now, we're leaving.'

'And we are,' Temple said, still smiling and holding his hands wide, 'but we are still going after Denver together.'

Jack sighed and looked aloft a moment. 'You can't make us join you.'

Temple removed his smile. 'Then I'll just have to talk to — '

'And don't bother threatening us with Sheriff Mitchell again. If you want to talk to the law, do that, but his deputy let us go, and I reckon he'll do the same.'

'You're wrong. Mitchell is tougher than that deputy in Bluff Creek. He's sure to find something to charge you with.' Temple glanced around, confirming that nobody was close to their end of the bar, but he still lowered his voice as he drew them into a huddle. 'But don't worry. I just want you to take me to where you found that money. After that, if you don't want to take on Denver, I'll go after him on my own.'

Jack glanced at Emmet and Emmet gave a resigned shrug. So, they headed out of the saloon.

With darkness having descended,

they were too late to ride out to the place where Jack had claimed they'd found the money. So Temple offered to let them sleep on his floor for the night before heading out at first light the next day. With mounting apprehension, they rode out of town.

On the way to Temple's house Jack and Emmet flashed glances at each other as they silently debated how they could avoid making this journey. The only plan Jack could think of was to sneak away when Temple was asleep. But that uninspired plan looked doomed to fail and he couldn't help but feel that ever since they'd stolen the gold, events were following an inevitable and probably disastrous path.

When they reached Temple's house, two miles out of Stonewall, Jack was too depressed to question the fact that four horses were outside the house and that a light was on inside from where subdued chatter was emerging.

His mood hadn't lightened when Temple led them in and he saw that four men were standing around the room. From the eager way they eyed them he reckoned they had been awaiting their arrival.

Only when Temple darted in and whipped their guns from their holsters did he snap into realizing the danger they were in, but by then it was too late.

'Now,' Temple said, throwing their guns through the door, 'you two just told me a mighty interesting story. Trouble is, I don't believe a word of it. So, I'll leave you to tell your story to these men.'

Temple gestured at the nearest man, grinding a fist into his palm, then slipped away through the door, leaving Jack and Emmet alone with four heavily set and armed men. Unbidden, Jack and Emmet backed away as the men paced towards them, cutting off their only escape route.

'What you want us to say?' Emmet whined.

The nearest man cracked his knuckles. 'Everything.'

'But we got nothing to add to what we told Temple.'

The man snorted and slapped a firm hand on Emmet's shoulder.

'Then this is going to be a very long and very painful night for you.'

★　★　★

Sheriff Mitchell looked up from considering the gold bar on his desk as Deputy Temple Kelly headed into the jailhouse.

'Where are they?' he asked.

'I didn't believe their story,' Temple said. 'So the boys have taken them out of town to see if they can beat anything more out of them.'

'And what story did they tell?'

'They're harmless brothers. They found a gold bar and some money on the trail in Broken Rock Canyon. Their youngest brother went wild, drew the attention of the wrong man, and got himself killed. Denver Calhoun was there and saved the other two.'

Mitchell picked up the bar and lay it flat on his palm.

'And who has the other gold bar?'

'Deputy Fairborn.'

Mitchell nodded. 'When this is over I guess I'll have to recruit me another deputy.'

'I guess. But I did learn something mighty interesting and it makes me think that some of what they said was true because they didn't know its significance.' Temple raised his eyebrows. 'Denver Calhoun has got himself a new partner — Rico Warren.'

Mitchell darted his gaze up. 'Now there's a name I haven't heard in a while.'

'And that points to one man — Flynn. Except Rico would never betray Flynn, but he has. Maybe the thought of gold has chewed away at his mind.'

Mitchell waggled a finger. 'Just because it looks like that, it doesn't mean he has.'

Temple sat on the edge of Mitchell's

desk and pointed at the bar.

'You should still consider the possibility. Keeping that bar in full view is mighty tempting.'

Mitchell nodded. 'Who don't you trust?'

'Everybody.' Temple smiled. 'Including myself.'

'Then you'll be pleased to know I trust you even more than you do.' Mitchell sighed and stood, hefting the bar. 'But you're right. I'll put it somewhere safe and out of sight.'

Mitchell took the bar to the armoury. He unlocked and opened the door, took the rifles out and leaned them against the wall, leaving the interior bare. Then he hooked two short and bent lengths of steel into slots on either side of the wooden bottom and lifted it out.

Beneath the false bottom was a ledge and he placed the gold bar in the centre beside the three other identical gold bars.

Then he replaced the bottom and the rifles, and locked the door.

6

The wrecked wagon had lain at the bottom of the canyon for at least a day. The gouged track down the side of the canyon showed its fate and a second intact wagon suggested that a group had located it later.

The sprawling mass of bullet-ridden bodies confirmed that a pitched battle had then taken place.

'You expecting to see this?' Denver asked, reluctantly accepting that this discovery proved that Rico had told the truth.

Rico hunched forward in the saddle.

'I ain't too surprised,' he said, his low voice sounding more honest than at any time since they had formed their partnership.

Denver nodded, then set Rico to work. While Rico rounded up the stray horses Denver gathered the bodies together. As the buzzards' feasting had ensured that identification was difficult, Denver tried to piece together what had happened from the location of the bodies.

He reckoned one group had been with the wagon that had tumbled down the side of the canyon. The other group had ambushed them. The ambushers had lost many men, but so had the ambushed group.

In fact, the fatalities were so high that Denver couldn't tell which group could deem themselves to have won, although as he found prints that headed away, clearly somebody had survived to leave.

Denver gathered his wanted posters of Flynn's gang and wandered from body to body, trying to match a picture to the bloated and torn faces. But nobody had ever got close enough to get a good description of any of Flynn's gang and Flynn himself had no description at all.

And even if he had had a likeness to

match, the bodies were too ravaged for Denver to know for sure what any of them looked like when alive — except for one. He was Deputy Luther Miles from Bent Knee — one of Sheriff Mitchell's many deputies.

This body lay further up the slope and, from its broken bones, Denver reckoned he was the wagon driver. This presumption didn't help to clarify what had happened here and he decided to load all the bodies on to the intact wagon and take them back to Bluff Creek for identification — and collection of any bounty.

As Rico hitched two horses up to the wagon Denver placed Luther's body on the wagon, then gestured at the row of bodies.

'Recognize anyone?' he asked.

Rico walked along the row, shaking his head, although his occasional raised eyebrow or flinch suggested to Denver that he did recognize some of them. Finally, he reached the end of the line and returned to Denver.

'Some of these were with Flynn,' he reported.

'Any of them Flynn himself?'

Rico glanced around, his nose wrinkled with contempt and the smell.

'After feeding the buzzards there's no way of knowing for sure.'

'Then you're of no use to me no more. Once we get back to Bluff Creek, you can rest up in the jailhouse.'

'Hey,' Rico whined. 'You still need me.'

'I don't. This ambush ended your usefulness and I got no need to keep you out of jail.' Denver provided a wide smile. 'Unless you want to tell me something else.'

Rico paced away from the bodies and leaned on the wagon beside Denver. He took a deep breath.

'You reckon you're an honourable man?' he asked, his tone sounding honest enough to intrigue Denver.

'More than most.'

'That ain't enough. I want some assurance you'll let me go if I tell you everything.'

'And you won't get it.' Denver aimed a firm finger at Rico. 'But I'll tell you this: you know something and unless you talk, I will take you back to Bluff Creek and let the law deal with you as a member of Flynn's gang.'

Rico looked away from Denver and down the canyon.

'Then I guess I got to tell you, for all the good it'll do you if you do double-cross me.' Rico paced around in a circle, stopping when he faced Denver. 'When you burst into my house, Flynn had left. He was heading here to . . . to collect something and was planning to hole up at that cave.' He gestured all around him. 'This ambush shows why he never got there.'

'And what was the something he was to collect?'

Rico lowered his head, murmuring to himself and Denver reckoned he was concocting a feeble lie, but the answer when it came had the sound of truth.

'Gold bars,' he said, looking up, 'one hundred, maybe more.'

'And who did he plan to steal it from?'

'Nobody.' Rico rubbed his jaw, frowning. 'Well, not exactly.'

Rico sighed, then veered on a path around various bodies, pausing a moment to look down at them, then move on. He reached the rim leading to a hollow and looked up at the wrecked wagon, shaking his head.

Denver judged that for all Rico's faults, people he knew had died here and he let him wander, but when he circled back towards him, he stood before him.

'Seen enough? Ready to talk?'

Rico sighed and hunched his shoulders.

'The gold bars were an old bounty, the biggest there has ever been,' he said, his voice low and defeated. 'Nobody will care that it's gone missing because nobody knows that it has or will even admit it ever existed. It was supposed to be a bounty on Santa Ana's head, but when he hightailed it back to Mexico, it quietly disappeared. Then it surfaced a few weeks back and a whole heap of people have been trying to get their hands on it.' Rico turned to look at the long row of bodies. 'And they'll do anything to get it.'

Denver nodded. 'A one-hundred-gold-bar bounty is enough to turn anyone's mind. Obliged for the truth, at last.'

'And what you planning to do with that truth?'

'Nothing. We're still heading to Bluff Creek with these bodies.' Denver paused a moment to consider Rico. 'But I won't be visiting no jailhouse.'

'Obliged for that, but what about the gold?'

'Don't care about that,' Denver said. 'I'm a bounty hunter, not an outlaw. These bodies are my gold.'

'But there's a huge pile of real gold out there somewhere, and nobody cares that it's gone missing. There's plenty of tracks leading away. We could follow them and see where they lead.'

'We could but we ain't. Someone else

can have the gold. I just want my bounty.' Denver headed to the first body and stood over it. 'Unless you can convince me that Flynn is still alive and has the gold.'

'I can't prove that.'

Denver shrugged, then looked up, planning to order Rico to help him carry the bodies to the wagon. But he saw movement nearby and glanced to the side.

Rico followed Denver's gaze to see that around a dozen men were heading down the snaking extent of the river and straight towards them.

Even as he was looking to Denver for advice, the leading men tore out their guns and blasted a volley of gunfire.

Denver and Rico stood a moment, but when lead whistled through the air around them, they scurried for cover.

★   ★   ★

Jack crawled over the hard ground to sit beside Emmet, who peered back at him, flexing his bruised and blood-streaked jaw.

'You all right?' Jack asked.

'Do I look all right?' Emmet murmured, prodding at his ribs and wincing.

'Nope.' Jack forced a hollow and unconvincing chuckle.

'And for that matter, neither do you.'

Jack grunted and lay on his back beside Emmet.

Several hours had passed since the beating had ended and, with the sun now lightening the horizon, Jack consoled himself with the fact that they'd survived to see another day. It'd take some fortitude to drag their battered bodies to a safe place to rest up, but at least they had that chance. Last night he'd doubted that they would.

The men Temple had left them with had pummelled and questioned them with a single-minded devotion to uncovering the truth.

Jack had rapidly decided that he no longer wanted anything to do with the gold and would have revealed every snippet of information about it if he'd thought it would stop the beating. But as he hadn't thought they'd survive, he'd kept to their version of their tale.

Emmet had also been resilient enough to avoid telling the men what had really happened. But under their systematic assault he had provided them with additional details: the chase, the wagon tumbling down into Broken Rock Canyon, the fact that they'd found the gold and money in the wagon.

The men had no inkling that there might be more gold and as the location was familiar to them and they reckoned a wagon could have fallen there, they'd appeared convinced that they'd heard the truth.

Still, they went through the story again, rechecking every detail and accompanying every falter or hint of duplicity with another round of battering.

Finally they'd relented and late into

the night, they'd taken them to a location five miles out of town. There, they'd stolen their money, leaving them with only the clothes they wore and their horses along with orders that they should never return to Stonewall.

Then they'd galloped off into the night, presumably to find the wagon in Broken Rock Canyon.

Before passing out into a mixture of sleep and blessed unconsciousness, both men had deemed themselves more than lucky.

'Where's the next nearest town?' Jack asked.

'Don't care,' Emmet said, slapping a fist on the ground then standing. 'I've had enough of this. Everything went wrong when we found that gold.'

Jack sat up. 'You ain't getting no argument there, but I guess we got lucky. We're still alive and that's better off than Horace is.'

Emmet staggered round on the spot to look down at Jack.

'And for how much longer? We've

been fated ever since we stole that gold. We look for fun. People come looking to kill us. We look for a quiet life. People come looking to kill us. If we leave now, what will happen?'

Emmet threw his arms wide, but as Jack reckoned he didn't want an answer, he remained quiet. But he did lever himself to his feet then straighten out his stoop. He placed a hand on his brother's shoulder and nodded.

'They're precisely my thoughts, Emmet. Everything went wrong when we stole the gold. And I reckon as soon as we get to somewhere safe, we do the right thing and let someone in authority know about what we did.'

Emmet flinched back, knocking Jack's hand away.

'I was going to say that's exactly what we don't do. Everyone wants us dead whether we got the gold or not. So, I say we head back to that lake and dig it up, then try to spend it.'

'That'll just get us killed.'

'It might, but we might get lucky, and

I'd sooner have a chance of being rich and dead than die poor on the trail like we nearly did last night.'

Jack closed his eyes a moment. 'We ain't doing that.'

'You don't tell me what I do.'

Emmet took a belligerent pace towards Jack and stabbed a firm finger at his chest.

In Jack's weakened state, the force knocked him back a pace.

Jack righted himself. 'Somebody has to talk sense into you.'

'And that ain't you.' Emmet turned to his horse. 'And I sure as hell ain't getting myself half-killed again for that gold without getting a chance to spend it.'

Jack strode two shuffling paces and slammed a hand on Emmet's back. 'You ain't going.'

Emmet stomped to a halt and glared down at the hand without turning.

'You can't stop me.'

Jack tightened his grip. 'I will.'

For long moments they stood looking

in opposite directions.

'Jack, we're brothers,' Emmet said, his softer tone encouraging Jack to raise his hand and let him turn to face him.

'I guess we are. We don't have to argue about this.'

'We don't.' Emmet squared up to Jack, his eyes gleaming and his fists flexing. 'And after what we went through last night, don't make me hit you.'

Jack backed away a pace, collecting his thoughts, but despite his attempts to keep himself calm, blood was now pounding in his ears. A part of him knew he was angry about everything that had happened to them rather than Emmet's attitude, but that didn't stop him slamming his hands on his hips and glaring at Emmet.

'We've fought before, Emmet, and I had no trouble whupping you then.'

Emmet aped Jack's stance. 'Yeah, but when we fought it was over a game of cards or some damn fool nonsense, not over something important. You know

I'm right or you wouldn't have helped steal the gold. Now, come with me and we'll do what we should have done all along.'

'I'm going nowhere and neither are you.'

'Final word?'

'Final word.'

Emmet glanced at his fist, but then shook his head and lowered it. He turned and took a single pace towards his horse, but Jack thrust his head down and broke into a run.

Emmet heard him coming and stepped to the side but, after last night's punishment, he moved too slowly.

Jack slammed his shoulders into Emmet's side and carried him on until Emmet slipped and the two men rolled to the ground, floundering beneath Emmet's spooked horse.

They avoided the hoofs and rolled clear, but now all the pent-up worries of the last few days burst out as each man pummelled the other.

They rolled one way, then the other,

dust flying around them, only their aching muscles stopping them from inflicting too much damage on each other as they wrestled.

At last with an angry oath, Jack pushed Emmet away and they rolled clear of each other, then staggered to their feet. They circled, crouched and facing each other with their fists raised.

Emmet threw the first punch, but it whistled past a foot before Jack's nose. Jack saw Emmet wince as the force of the missed blow rocked him to the side, inflicting more damage on himself than he would have on Jack.

With their mutual lack of strength in mind, Jack beckoned him on, and Emmet again threw a punch. Again, it missed.

Jack taunted his brother and this time Emmet stormed in and threw a straight punch at him. Jack darted his head back, but he couldn't avoid this blow and it crunched into his chin.

After all the punishment they'd both received the previous night, the blow was soft and only jarred his head, but Jack, in his weakened state, slipped and tumbled on his back. On the ground, he shook himself and looked up to see that Emmet was taking a running dive at him.

Jack rolled out of the way and Emmet missed him, slamming into the earth with a pained screech.

From the corner of his eye Jack glanced at Emmet, who had curled up with his forehead pressed to the dirt, and Jack couldn't help but laugh. He slumped down to lie on his back looking skyward, listening to Emmet murmur and grunt to himself.

'We can't fight,' Jack said, the sudden burst of anger that had hit him evaporating. 'We just ain't got the strength.'

He turned to Emmet, smiling, hoping his brother would see sense, but then gulped when he saw that Emmet had rolled to his knees.

And he'd grabbed a rock in his right hand.

Jack just had time to flinch away, but by then Emmet was whirling the rock around and, with a dull crunch, it slammed into his forehead.

7

Denver faced at least a dozen advancing riders and, from their sustained gunfire, he reckoned they weren't looking to take him alive.

Having pinned down both himself and Rico behind the wagon, the men dismounted and hurried to cover, taking root behind rocks at the bottom of the canyon while some headed to higher ground to gain a different angle on them.

Denver had decided against running, figuring that a safe place in the stark and steep-sided canyon would be hard to find, and that the bounty of the dead men was large enough to fight for.

But pinned down behind the wagon, he realized that the bounty his attackers were fighting for was even more valuable — himself.

He expected that Rico would turn

against him and he spent as much time watching him as he did their assailants. But when Rico stood and looked around, perhaps with a view to letting the ambushers know it was he, gunfire exploded around him and forced him to drop to his knees.

'Finished giving them target practice?' Denver said.

'Just trying to see where they all are,' Rico said, crouching down.

'Of course you were. Now, if you keep your head down, I got a chance of getting us out of this alive.'

'That'll only happen if you give me back my gun.'

Denver was about to refuse, but then a sustained burst of gunfire exploded, gouging splinters out of the wagon above his head. He closed his eyes a moment, considering, then withdrew Rico's gun from his pocket and passed it over.

'Obliged,' Rico said, throwing open the chamber to confirm the gun was unloaded. 'What's the plan?'

Denver glanced around. The gently flowing river was fifty yards before him. A hollow where the broken wagon had collapsed was around the same distance behind him.

'First, we get better cover.'

Rico punched in the final bullet. 'And when we doing that?'

'Around about . . . Now!'

Denver leapt to his feet and pounded towards the hollow. Rico jumped up and followed him a moment later.

One of their assailants was seeking cover in a higher position and this man alerted the others with a shot that scythed several feet ahead of Denver. Firing sideways on the run, Denver returned fire.

As he was running and not taking care with his aim, Denver's first three shots were wild.

Emboldened, the man stood still and took careful aim. But before he could fire, Denver got in a lucky shot that ripped across his arm and Rico slid to a halt and tore a shot into his chest that threw him on his back.

Then they both concentrated on running, hurtling across the ground.

The other men stayed behind their cover, venturing up only when both men were around ten yards from the hollow. A huge volley of gunshots hurried them on and Denver dived the last few yards, rolling to a scrambling halt over the rim of the hollow.

Rico vaulted in after him, then rolled round to lie on his belly and quickly shuffled back to the rim, but Denver slapped him on his shoulder, pointed up the slope, then set off.

Rico stayed at the bottom a moment, then hurried after Denver.

Doubled up they reached the highest section of the hollow containing the broken wagon. There, Denver dropped to his belly and crawled to the side to take cover on a flat rock in front of a large boulder, from which he could see down into the hollow and along the slope beyond.

Rico crawled to the edge of the flat

rock, then stopped.

'You sure?' he said. 'This ain't exactly good cover.'

'I'm on high. That's the best place to be when we're this far outnumbered. You want to hide behind the wagon, do that.'

Rico wavered, then hurried back to roll into hiding behind the wagon. Denver didn't add that he hoped the ambushers would reckon they'd both hide behind the wagon and that his appearance here might surprise a few of them.

And sure enough, down below, a line of men shuffled into view, scurrying to seek cover beyond the rim, but also peering up at the wagon.

Denver had flashed views of their hats and backs, but he held his fire. Rico did not, loosing off several shots that kept them from coming over the rim, but which also confirmed where he was.

One of the men waved to someone out of Denver's view, and if that were a signal to outflank them, then the man was coming up on Denver's side of the hollow.

Denver removed his hat and slapped a quick dusting of dirt over his face, then lay as flat and as still as he could.

More signals passed from the man beyond the rim and even a few animal calls. Then they came.

Three men rolled over the rim, all keeping a low profile and scuttling for cover behind low rocks. Rico loosed off gunfire at them, his wild burst cannoning into the dirt or whistling through the air.

Denver kept still and Rico shot him a bemused glance, but Denver risked only a returned wink, then resumed watching what their assailants did.

And they were moving into place to attack the wagon. The three men at the bottom of the hollow fired up the slope, keeping Rico pinned down while three more men slipped over the rim and hurried to positions higher up the slope.

Beyond the hollow and to the side, three men darted between boulders, even though they were out of sight of the wagon as they gained a position where they could outflank them.

Denver presumed the remaining three men were carrying out a similar manoeuvre on the other side of the hollow. And it would be these men who would be the first to see that Denver had taken cover elsewhere.

Denver shuffled round to the side, still keeping the land below and to the side of the hollow in view while he waited until either he chose to reveal his position or the attackers forced him to.

Below him, the men were still advancing using the tactic of three men covering the other three as they moved to higher ground, then for those men to return the favour. Now they were twenty yards from the wagon and the possibility of their trading deadly gunfire within seconds had become a certainty.

The men to Denver's side had

climbed for the same distance up the slope and they swooped in. And Denver presumed the men on the other side were also about to pounce.

Still he hung on for a few more seconds, waiting until the three men below tried to reach their ultimate position. Then he bobbed up.

He'd mentally practised the action several times and he fired coolly and precisely, taking the first man through the chest, then moving on to hammer lead into the next men. Only the third man dived for cover, but he never reached it, a shot to the shoulders knocking him to his knees and a second shot to the side sending him rolling down the slope.

The gunfire from an unexpected position took the men outside the hollow by surprise. They skidded to a halt and ran for cover, but, with none of them covering another, Denver blasted a slug into one man's fleeing back and hurried the others on their way. He reloaded as Rico opened fire, although with everyone already behind cover it only had the effect of keeping them pinned down.

But then lead whistled past Denver's head, throwing grit from the ricochet up into his face. Denver flinched away from the shot, darting his gaze around for the shooter, but couldn't see where he was hiding.

He ran his gaze over the various covered positions again, then winced. He'd covered every angle — except one.

He rolled away; his action saved him from a bullet that crunched into the rock where his back had been a moment earlier, and stopped his roll with him lying on his back and his gun thrust skywards.

On the top of the boulder behind him a man was peering down at him — Denver wasn't the only one who'd thought of gaining cover in an unexpected place.

Denver tore off deadly gunfire straight up into the air, his shot winging into the man's forehead, knocking his head up before he came tumbling down. Denver rolled again to avoid the falling man, but even as he rolled, he realized that the dead man wasn't the only man coming down from above. And the other man was alive.

He halted and swung round but he was too late and a body slammed on to his back, pole-axing him.

Winded and flattened, Denver saw a flash of metal as his assailant arced a knife around and scythed the blade in towards his throat.

★ ★ ★

'You look like you've seen some trouble,' Sheriff Mitchell said as Jack Turner staggered into the jailhouse. 'You know who did it?'

Jack shuffled another pace, then headed for the nearest chair and slumped into it without Mitchell giving him permission.

He'd come to an hour ago to find

that his worst fears had been realized. Emmet had taken his horse, ensuring that he couldn't go after him, and also ensuring that he had no choice as to where he went.

So Jack had headed to Stonewall, unsure as to whether he could actually double-cross his own brother, but consoling himself with the thought that this was the only way for him to stop Emmet making a terrible mistake.

'Yeah,' Jack said, rubbing the back of his head, 'but that don't matter. I guess I had a good beating coming to me.'

'That's your decision, but if you don't help me, I can't do nothing to stop whoever did it from beating on other people.'

'I understand, but I'm not here about the beating. It's about this bounty hunt for Denver Calhoun.'

Mitchell sighed and waved in a dismissive gesture towards the door.

'Plenty of people have asked and I'll tell you what I told them — the bounty is one gold bar and you got to bring him to me to collect.' Mitchell eyed Jack's battered face and torn clothing. 'You reckon you're in a fit state to track down a man who killed the first two people who tried to bring him in?'

'I wouldn't go after Denver even if I were fit. He's an innocent man.'

'He killed the man who owned that gold bar and until I know why, he's under suspicion.' Mitchell narrowed his eyes, then nodded slowly. 'But if the information I've heard is correct, I know who you are. You're one of the men he saved in Bluff Creek.'

'I am,' Jack said, enjoying telling the truth for once and feeling his muscles relax as he started to unburden his woes on to the law. 'And I got more, but you got to accept my word when I say that nobody did wrong.'

'I'll decide that for myself. Just tell me everything.' Mitchell stared at Jack, his eyes cold, but when Jack didn't answer immediately, he flashed a smile. 'The truth never harms innocent men.'

'Suppose it doesn't. And I guess I

can't evade this any more.' Jack sighed and took a deep breath. 'Emmet, my brother, and me aren't outlaws, but we got caught up in something and the only way out is to do the right thing. And that's why I'm here. I got a story to tell and I've told a whole lot of versions of it already, but now I have to tell the truth. It all started when we saw this wagon heading along the top of Broken Rock Canyon.'

Mitchell's eyes gleamed as he leaned forward.

'Just tell me what happened next and you got nothing to worry about.'

8

The knife sliced in and Denver only had enough time to buck and squirm away, the knife sparking into the rock before his face.

But his assailant settled his weight down on Denver's back, then jerked the knife in towards Denver's right eye. Denver saw the point of the blade slashing closer, but then the knife fell from the man's grip, his fist brushing Denver's cheek before he fell away.

Denver then registered that he'd heard a nearby gunshot and that Rico must have saved him, but he didn't have time to waste on being relieved.

He bucked the shot man from his back, then rolled to his haunches. He couldn't see the men outside the hollow and that meant they must have found cover elsewhere. Denver shuffled back towards the boulder, then, bent double, ran for the wagon.

Rico saw him coming and helped him in with covering gunfire. Denver skidded to a halt beside him. He slammed his gun on the top of the wagon and loosed off a couple of shots, firing blind, then dropped to lean back against the wagon as he reloaded.

'Obliged,' he said.

'Don't know why I bothered,' Rico said. 'You left me here to draw their fire.'

'You chose to come here.' Denver shrugged. 'And besides, you used the position well.'

Rico uttered a snorting chuckle then glanced over the wagon. 'We've almost halved their numbers, but they won't make the same mistake again, and they got us pinned down here.'

Denver roved his gaze up the slope behind the wagon. The canyon became increasingly steep and it was unlikely that anyone could get much higher than they had and still have good cover.

'And worse,' he said, 'we don't know

where they all are any more.'

'You got another plan?'

'Nope, other than keep your head down and shoot at anyone who doesn't.'

Rico nodded, then shuffled down. Both men listened for any signs of their assailants approaching. But then a burst of gunfire came from on high, blasting down from behind the large boulder.

Both men shuffled round to face it as another volley exploded, and there was still no sign of exactly where it was coming from, but neither was it aimed at them.

Then Denver realized what was happening. He slapped Rico's arm, grinning, then rolled to his haunches and peered over the wagon.

Down below, one of their assailants was edging round his covering rock while firing up at the boulder. And enough of his attention was on the person he was aiming at to give Denver time to take aim and deliver a shot to the man's side that rocked him back on his heels.

Rico followed through with a shot that tore through the man's neck, wheeling him into the rock, where he lay sprawled with his arms dangling.

The other men stayed down, but Denver saw a man edge backwards to the top of the boulder. Then gunfire exploded and the man hurtled downward with his limbs splayed and his chest holed, to land on his back. He writhed a moment, then flopped and stilled.

'We got help,' Rico said beside him. Denver confirmed his simple declaration with a contented nod. 'But how many?'

'That ain't as important a question as how do we help them — or him — out?'

Rico nodded and, with the ambushers staying down, they slipped away from the wagon and hurried towards higher ground. The men walked sideways with their backs to each other, covering the ground on either side as they waited for anyone to show themselves.

And when they did, it came with a low whistle to Denver's side and from the top of the boulder. A short wave from their saviour confirmed that it was Deputy Fairborn and they quickly skirted round the boulder to gain its top and join him.

They didn't waste time on acknowledgements, instead edging to the sides of the boulder to hunker down in three different positions. Then they started up a persistent bombardment of the remaining positions, their gunfire being accurate enough to keep the attackers from returning anything other than sporadic retorts.

And when Rico delivered a sharp shot to one man who bobbed up, the others lost heart. After one last sustained burst of gunfire that forced Denver and the others to dive for cover, Denver bobbed up to see a ragged line of men hurtling away down the slope for their horses.

The three defenders jumped to their feet and ensured that they kept running with a volley of shots at their backs. Although all their shots were wild, none of the men so much as looked back as they gained their horses, then galloped away along the side of the river.

While Denver and Fairborn hurried off in opposite directions, checking various positions to ensure that the men's flight was what it seemed, Rico examined the bodies.

When Denver had accounted for all of the men who had attacked him he returned to the hollow to find that Rico had riffled through the belongings of the bodies and had collected a thick pile of wanted posters.

'Hey, Denver,' he shouted, looking up. 'You got to see this.'

But Denver didn't need to. From Rico's grin, he reckoned every single poster had his face on it.

★　★　★

Hunched forward in the saddle, Jack Turner considered the trail ahead.

At his side was a large cage on a wagon, either to secure prisoners or to carry the gold. And trailing behind him were Sheriff Mitchell and several of the least reputable-looking deputies Jack had ever seen.

Temple Kelly was amongst them, perpetually grinning at Jack, and the revelation that this untrustworthy man was a deputy had done nothing to lighten Jack's mood.

But despite his misgivings, Jack never strayed from his course, going directly to the lake where he and Emmet had buried the gold. He was sure they both faced lengthy jail sentences, and that Emmet would never forgive him. But he reckoned that, faced with such a bad situation, handing over the gold to the law was the least worst thing he could do.

So, as they neared Broken Rock Canyon, he tried to convince himself that he wasn't double-crossing his brother, but saving him from suffering the same fate as Horace had suffered.

However hard he tried, his efforts didn't cheer him.

Mitchell didn't question his directions and, five miles away from Broken Rock Canyon, Jack stopped the group.

When he and his brothers had stolen the gold, they had rested on a ridge overlooking a lake and discussed what to do. When they'd decided to bury the gold, they'd chosen a spot in the forest beside the lake.

Emmet had several hours on them and, as it should have taken him only an hour or so to dig up the gold, Jack was concerned that they wouldn't reach him in time. But he kept those fears to himself.

They rode beneath the ridge, then veered off into the forest, taking the same route the brothers had taken earlier. They had been worried that they might not return for several years and they'd chosen a route that they could remember even if trees fell and the landscape subtly changed.

They followed a creek, then stopped at an arrangement of rocks, the tapering end of the outermost rock pointing them towards their final destination. From here, they'd taken fifty paces, but even standing by the rock, Jack could see the fresh mound of earth.

Sheriff Mitchell and his deputies headed away to stand over the hole. They glared at the fresh earth then at a scraping track in the ground, which provided final confirmation that Emmet had removed the box before leaving. Then they traipsed off, searching for his trail, while Jack sat on the tapering rock.

Within a few minutes, Deputy Temple Kelly found a trail. He led them off in the precise direction Jack had expected Emmet to have gone — towards the lake.

Jack figured that Emmet wouldn't have expected to have been found so quickly. And he wasn't impetuous, so that meant he'd rest up for a while and perhaps even sleep on what his next decision should be.

And so, when they closed on the lake and the trees thinned, Jack wasn't surprised to see a solitary figure sitting beside the water. He sat on a small promontory of land that thrust into the lake — a location where the brothers had often fished. He was crouched over a log, with two other logs lying to his side.

Mitchell suggested that Emmet was building a barrier for a fire and although Jack thought this unlikely, he didn't argue. But when he saw that Emmet had obtained a gun, he did face up to Mitchell.

'I'll talk to him,' he said.

'You won't,' Mitchell said, looking over Jack's shoulder towards the lake. 'This is a task for the law.'

'Remember what I said. Emmet ain't a bad man, but he's scared. He might overreact when he sees you, and if he starts shooting — '

Mitchell raised a hand silencing him.

'If he starts shooting, we won't return fire. That satisfy you?'

Jack nodded. 'Obliged.'

Mitchell patted Jack's shoulder, then directed his deputies with silent gestures before turning back to Jack.

'Now, keep your head down and let us do this.' Mitchell smiled. 'Trust me.'

Jack did as Mitchell ordered and stayed down, but he secured a position where he could watch Emmet so that if he did act aggressively, he could shout down at him to give himself up.

But Mitchell took no chances as he moved his deputies steadily in to surround Emmet. One man headed along the side of the lake to Emmet's right and another went to Emmet's left. Then the other deputies spread out and moved down the slope towards him, darting between boulders and outlying trees as they closed.

With all of Emmet's attention being on whatever he was building, he didn't look back, and when Mitchell took up a closer position on the edge of the treeline, Jack ignored his instructions and followed.

From closer to, he saw that Emmet wasn't building something but was dismantling his work, and the nearest deputy had paced quietly to within twenty paces of Emmet's back. Emmet sat, steadily working and seemingly unaware of the approaching man, who paced again, placing his feet to the ground with steady care.

Pace by pace he closed, but then rocked to a halt, his sudden gesture suggesting to Jack that he'd made a noise.

And sure enough, Emmet straightened, then swirled round, scrambling for his gun, but the deputy dived for cover behind a rock. Then the deputy who had closed to within thirty yards of Emmet's side fired a warning shot over Emmet's head.

Emmet rolled forwards over the logs to lie on the other side, facing up the slope.

'Emmet Turner,' Mitchell shouted

from his position behind a pine. 'This is Sheriff Mitchell. Throw down your gun. We got you surrounded.'

'You'll have to come here and get me,' Emmet shouted.

'You'll surrender first.'

Emmet bobbed up to dart his gaze around, then dived for cover.

'I'll take my chances.'

Jack had heard enough of Emmet's bravado and he stood, then paced down the slope. Beside him, Mitchell swirled round, gesturing wildly, but Jack swung to the side to avoid him.

Mitchell barked desperate orders at him to not show himself, but Jack was determined to avoid taking orders where his brother's safety was concerned.

'Emmet,' he shouted, emerging from the trees, 'it's me, Jack. Give yourself up.'

'What you done to me, Jack?' Emmet shouted.

'I've saved you from making a terrible mistake.'

'But you've set the law on me.'

'I ain't proud of myself, but you gave me no choice.' Jack bounded down the last few yards of the slope then paced to a halt on flat ground in front of the lake, about ten yards from Emmet. He spread his hands. 'I've lost one brother because of that gold and I ain't losing another.'

'You're the one who's set guns on me.'

'Law guns.' Jack turned on the spot, pointing out the various positions of Mitchell and his deputies. 'We've both seen what the thought of gold does to a man's mind, and nobody will rest until they can take it from you. The only way you'll get out of this alive is if you hand it over. So, do what Sheriff Mitchell said and throw down your gun.'

Emmet murmured to himself, then ventured a glance over his log, confirming that the deputies were staying down before he looked at Jack.

'And then what?'

'And then we'll both go to jail, I

guess, but that won't be as bad as if we'd tried to escape with the gold. We'll be alive and when we get out, we can go back to doing what we're good at — hunting and fishing and trading furs and — '

'And I reckon I'll take my chances with the gold.' Emmet pointed a firm finger up the slope, then shuffled down behind the log with the gun planted firmly on the wood. 'Now, step away. You ain't the only one who doesn't want to lose another brother.'

'Emmet,' Jack said, taking a slow and deliberate pace towards him. 'You can't take Sheriff Mitchell and his deputies on. Remember, we couldn't even face down one card-shark when we outnumbered him three to one.'

'He was a fast draw, but I got some motivation now. And you will stop right there!'

Jack advanced another pace. 'Then you'll just have to shoot me because I ain't backing away.'

Jack continued his steady pacing, his

brother slowly coming into view behind the log. His gun was steady as he aimed up at Jack but behind the gun, his eyes were wide and pleading. Despite the lure of the gold, Jack couldn't believe Emmet would actually shoot him and he took another determined pace to stand square up to the log and looking down at him.

'Jack!' Emmet snapped. 'Stay back!'

Jack placed his foot on the log, rested his elbow on the raised knee, and held out his hand, palm up.

'Time to do the right thing, Emmet.' He smiled. 'Believe me. You'll feel better once you do.'

Emmet and Jack exchanged a lengthy stare, but Emmet was the first to look away. He released the hammer then opened his hand to let his gun swing down on his trigger-finger. Then he shuffled it back into his hand and placed it on Jack's palm.

'I just hope you're right about this, Jack, or I'll never forgive you, not ever.'

'And I know that,' Jack said. He

stood tall then held out his other hand to Emmet, who took it, and he levered him to his feet.

Emmet and Jack stood side by side as Sheriff Mitchell and his deputies rose from behind their cover and paced towards them. Jack patted Emmet's hunched back.

'What you want me to do now?' Emmet murmured.

'Tell the full truth, leaving nothing out. Then the gold can go back to its rightful owners and we can start living again.'

'It can,' Mitchell said, joining Jack. He took the gun from him then gestured for Jack to back away and for Emmet to kneel. While Temple frisked him, he turned to Jack. 'You did well. I reckoned we'd struggle to take him alive.'

'Like I said — there was no need for no shooting. Emmet ain't no outlaw. Neither of us will give you any trouble and we'll co-operate fully.'

Mitchell nodded and paced on a tour

around Emmet's campsite. Already Jack could see that the gold wasn't in an obvious place, and he guessed that Emmet had reburied it — although, as it turned out, not all of it.

When Mitchell directed two deputies to riffle through Emmet's belongings, they found a single gold bar. With the bar raised aloft, Mitchell returned to face Jack.

'I'll believe you ain't no outlaws,' he said, 'but that still leaves the question of where the rest of the gold is. Do you want to ask him where it is, or shall I?'

Jack thanked Mitchell for the opportunity and turned to his brother, who was kneeling with his hands thrust high, as Temple searched him.

'I ain't got it,' Emmet said, shaking his head.

'Emmet,' Jack urged, 'tell Mitchell everything, like I said. Keeping anything back will get us a real long stretch in prison.'

'I don't know nothing about no gold,' Emmet said with a defiant tilt to his chin despite the gold bar Mitchell was clutching.

Jack glared hard at Emmet, unable to form the words that'd persuade him he was acting foolishly, but behind him Mitchell snorted, then pushed him aside.

'You've had your chance to volunteer information,' he grunted. 'Now, you don't get a second chance.'

'Hey,' Jack said, 'ain't no need for no threats. I'll talk him round, like I talked him into giving up his gun.'

'And I ain't got time to waste.' Mitchell loomed over Emmet and thrust the gold bar under his nose. 'Talk. Now.'

Emmet glanced at the bar then folded his arms.

'I don't know nothing about nothing.'

Mitchell continued to glare at Emmet, but when Emmet returned that glare, he gestured to two of his deputies, who moved in and grabbed Emmet from behind and pulled him to his feet.

Jack swirled round to confront Mitchell, but Temple paced in and grabbed him from behind. He struggled, but cold metal jabbed into the base of his neck and he heeded the urgent demand that he be still.

The fact that Temple would turn a gun on Jack made Emmet's eyes open wide. He murmured a plea for Mitchell to give him time to think, but the sheriff had his back to him and was gesturing to his other deputies.

'Raise that log and drive it into the ground,' he ordered, 'then tie him to it.'

Emmet screeched and struggled, but one deputy cuffed him and the other held him securely.

'Hey,' Jack shouted, 'you got no need to punish him. I can persuade him to talk.'

Mitchell paced up to Jack, looked him up and down, and sneered.

'Don't want that. I want to trust the story I hear, and I reckon a little persuasion will do that.'

'I came to you because — '

Jack grunted, as Mitchell's back-handed cuff split his lip. The blow dragged him away from Temple's grip, but Temple moved in and clubbed him to his knees. Jack stared at the ground a moment then rolled to his feet, his fists rising, but only walked into an uppercut to the chin that stood him straight before he tumbled to the dirt.

He lay, rubbing his chin, as Mitchell issued brisk orders to his deputies to drag him away and secure him while they questioned Emmet.

As firm hands dragged him away from the lakeside, Jack shot Emmet a pleading glance, demanding that he co-operate, but Emmet shook his head.

Temple tied Jack to a tree about thirty yards away from the lake where he could see everything that happened. When his bonds were secure and Temple left him, Jack shouted to Emmet to talk, but this only had the effect of getting him gagged.

And then he could only watch.

Despite Sheriff Mitchell's sudden

brutality and his knowledge of Temple's methods, Jack couldn't believe they would do anything but scare Emmet. Mitchell was a sheriff, after all.

This view strengthened as Mitchell took a long time to prepare for his questioning. After two deputies had secured Emmet to the stake, he gathered his deputies around him, lit a fire, and even shared out the food they'd brought.

Jack received a portion before Temple replaced the gag and they even offered their food to Emmet, but he declined.

An hour passed with none of the lawmen even looking at Emmet.

As their silent method was similar to the method Deputy Fairborn had used on them when they were in a cell, Jack relaxed. He was even unconcerned when Mitchell left the fire to stand before Emmet.

The sheriff cocked his head to one side while considering his prisoner, but Emmet just returned his gaze, so Mitchell gestured over his shoulder.

He must have prearranged the gesture because two deputies gathered around the fire. Using a combination of scuffing feet and unburnt branches, they kicked the fire closer to Emmet, who broke his silence.

'What you doing?' he wailed.

Mitchell didn't answer, but he did gesture to a deputy, who knelt before Emmet and removed his boots.

Emmet shot a glance up the slope at Jack, his scared eyes asking whether Mitchell would really torture him.

Jack wanted to shake his head, but as the deputy bared Emmet's feet and Temple withdrew a flaming branch from the fire, Jack couldn't provide any assurance that he wouldn't.

9

'Obliged for your help,' Denver said when Deputy Fairborn and Rico had confirmed that they were now safe.

'You didn't really doubt I'd help you, did you?' Rico said.

'Sure did.' Denver glanced at Rico's gun. 'And I got to say you're a fair shot.'

Rico shrugged. 'A man's got to defend himself.'

'He has.' Denver turned to Fairborn. 'But I never expected to see you out here defending us.'

'Just sorry I was lagging so far behind,' Fairborn said.

'Those poker-players tell you about this place?'

'No. They were lying, so I released them to see where they went. They headed to Stonewall, these men bush-whacked them, and they nearly paid with their lives. But they must have talked because those men headed here. I followed them and it just so happens you were here already.'

Fairborn raised his eyebrows inviting an explanation of how Denver had found the scene of this wrecked wagon. Denver glanced at Rico, who was biting his bottom lip, perhaps in concern as to what Denver would reveal about him, and after Rico's help, Denver considered what he'd say before replying.

'Got to tell you the truth, Alan,' he said. 'I lied to you before. And I'm sorry for that.'

Fairborn shrugged. 'Got no problem with that. You hunt for bounty and sometimes that means you don't tell the law everything.'

'Yeah, but I don't usually keep outlaws out of jail.'

'Denver,' Rico urged.

Denver paced to the side and laid a hand on Rico's shoulder.

'Rico here ain't exactly my partner,

but I now believe he wasn't exactly an outlaw either. He didn't mind too much who stayed at his house, if you know what I mean.'

'I guess I do,' Fairborn said, looking at Rico. 'That include Flynn?'

'Yeah,' Rico said, looking away from both men, 'but I didn't get involved in what he was doing.'

'Can't say how bad that is for you, but if what I think Denver is saying is right and you've been co-operating, that'll work in your favour.'

Denver slapped a firm hand on Rico's back, pushing him forwards.

'So,' he said, 'as long as you keep remembering whose side you're on, we can all get on just fine and work together.'

Rico grumbled, but then snapped his head up.

'That mean you're not taking those bodies in for the bounty, but going after the gold?'

'I guess it does. If these men were just after me, there won't be no bounty on them. And I'm getting to think the men who died in the first attack won't have much value either. And that means I got to go after Flynn and the gold.'

'You've found out about the gold?' Fairborn asked and, to his increasingly incredulous bemusement, Denver outlined Rico's theory about the gold being an old bounty that had recently resurfaced.

When Denver had finished his tale, they wasted little time on discussion, agreeing that whether this tale was true or not, it was likely that the only men to have escaped from this ambush were Flynn and his gang.

They headed to their horses and scouted around. A tangle of prints was all round the site, but they unravelled one set which headed to the river and, on the other side, trailed away to the side of the canyon, then to a pass. Here, Fairborn announced that he could discern two separate trails, with the second group following the first. This fact was enticing enough for them to leave the canyon.

But once they were out on to the plains the first trail disappeared, suggesting that its makers had covered their tracks, and the other trail took a meandering route. They surmised that the following group had also lost the other's trail and had scouted around, trying to pick it up.

Eventually these tracks stopped at a camp; the remnants of the fire were still warm, implying they had moved on within the day. Then the trail veered away from a lake and headed broadly back towards Broken Rock Canyon.

None of the group was sure as to whether this sudden change of direction meant that the men they were following had picked up the original trail, or whether they had given up. But they all agreed upon one thing.

They were getting close to Flynn and the gold.

★　★　★

Emmet's screams were becoming increasingly pitiful.

Jack had worn his wrists ragged as he tried to free himself, but the bonds were still as secure as ever. And he didn't bother trying to shake away his gag so that he could shout at Emmet to answer Mitchell's questions because the sheriff wasn't asking any.

But his deputies were getting down to their serious, and apparently, familiar work of breaking Emmet's spirit.

Jack had thought that the previous night had been bad, but that was as nothing compared to the deputies' sustained and mutilating brutality, and he saw no hope of them surviving to see another day.

With fiendish delight, Temple had thrust lighted brands under Emmet's feet, and the screeches with which Emmet rent the air chilled Jack's blood. But that was just the start.

While a deputy heated a knife, Mitchell amused himself by firing at Emmet, aiming bullets around his form on the stake, each shot getting closer and closer until he was nicking the flesh. Then the deputy had set the red-hot knife to Emmet's bare chest, the stench of cooked meat making Jack retch against his gag.

All the time Sheriff Mitchell paced back and forth, his calm demeanour driving away all thoughts that he was anything other than the worst kind of lawman. And Jack had to accept that he'd made a terrible mistake in putting his trust in this man.

Jack tore his head to the side to avoid looking at Emmet, but each new scream forced him to glance at him. Each time he steeled himself, hoping that Emmet was overreacting, but on seeing each new burn, and later, the blood flowing as they set about skinning him alive, those thoughts fled.

But as the day wore on, a new thought pounded in his mind. He had to escape and help Emmet. And in that, he had one hope — all the deputies were working on their prisoner and their attention was on him.

He blocked out Emmet's cries of pain and forced himself to think logically. Temple had tied him to a tree with his hands behind his back. The bonds were too tight for him to release himself, but the rope wasn't thick.

And that meant he might be able to tease the strands of twine apart.

So, he stood and, as nobody was looking at him, settled his stance. With his hands being higher up the tree, the bonds weren't as tight as they were around the base of the tree and he could rub the rope up and down.

But after several minutes, he accepted that the soft bark would never wear through the rope. He needed something sharper.

He glanced down. Stones of various shapes and sizes were at his feet. He slipped down to sit and shuffled his feet through the stones, finding several that had sharp edges, then kicked them to the base of the trunk.

He checked that the lawmen were

still ignoring him, then slipped around the trunk and placed them with his hands behind his back. He grabbed two, one in each hand, then shuffled round to assume his former position.

Then he rocked his wrists back and forth across the length of rope he could reach. He couldn't tell whether the sharp ends were scything through the twine or whether he was wasting his time, and long minutes passed with the only result being the crippling cramps that grabbed his wrists.

But whenever he tired and the hopelessness of his escape attempt threatened to overwhelm him, Emmet would scream again and drive the pain from his thoughts.

Despite his resolution, his left hand tired first, but as he flexed the wrist, a better idea came to him. He fingered the bark until he found a knurl then slipped the stone into it, sharp side outermost, and scraped the rope up and down over the stone.

He was tempted to do the same with

his other hand, but didn't want to risk dislodging the stone now that he reckoned he was making progress for the first time.

And, in encouragement, he felt the rope give a mite. He redoubled his efforts, but his squirming was vigorous enough to attract Sheriff Mitchell's attention and he turned from the stake and headed towards him. ·

Jack stopped moving, then realized that his sudden stillness appeared even more suspicious. He shot a glance at Emmet, seeing with a gut-churning glance that one of the deputies had bound Emmet's left hand to the stake and was now chortling as he prised his fingernails away.

Jack offered a silent prayer that he would soon be able to help him and, without moving his body, he rocked his wrist up and down over the stone behind the tree, feeling the rope give again.

Mitchell continued to pace towards him and Jack fixed him with his glare, willing him to stop walking and not discover what he was doing.

'You looking forward to your turn?' Mitchell grunted.

Jack raised his chin. 'If it stops you hurting my brother, yes.'

'Brave talk.' Mitchell stopped before him and stood with one leg thrust out, his chin high and arrogant.

'Anyone can be brave when facing scum like you.' Then, seeing that Mitchell wasn't immediately about to check his bonds, Jack attempted to distract him by launching a tirade of abuse.

Mitchell listened to the abuse with his only reaction being a smile and raised eyebrows.

'You got some fire,' he said when Jack had quietened. 'That'll help keep your strength when we get to work on you.'

Jack felt the rope loosen a mite more. 'Why are you doing this?'

'For the gold. I've searched for it for years, picking up clues here and there, chasing rumours, and nobody will keep me from it now.'

Jack nodded down the slope at the stake. 'And you could have had it without doing this to Emmet.'

'When you've searched for as long as I have, you don't take risks. Soon, he'll answer any question to make me stop.' Mitchell chuckled. 'And if the gold is close, I might just do that.'

The rope loosened again and slipped down the tree behind Jack's back, making him feel that in another minute, perhaps less, he would free himself.

'Where did the gold come from?' he blurted, desperate to keep Mitchell talking for just a few more seconds.

'Flynn raided the bank in Bent Knee, but he didn't notice the gold buried in the cellar. My deputy did and he brought the gold to Stonewall, one bar at time, but that took time and one bar went missing. So, I ordered him to bring it all out in one go, but too much information had got out already. Flynn raided the convoy in Broken Rock Canyon. I still might have got the gold, but I couldn't have foreseen one small problem — the Turner brothers happening along.'

'But you're a lawman. You can't do . . . do this.'

'But I am.' Mitchell rocked his head to the side. 'And you're a man who is moving far too much for a bound man. Time to retie those bonds.'

Jack accepted that hiding what he was doing was no longer any use. He yanked his arm up and down behind his back, making the most of his last scrapes along the sharp stone, the motion so vigorous it knocked the stone to the ground.

But he felt the rope give again and he bunched his muscles as Mitchell leaned in towards him.

Then he yanked his arms apart. The rope gave far more readily than he expected and his arms came hurtling outwards, tumbling him forward. As he fell, he lunged out from the tree, bundling into Mitchell and grabbing for his gun.

Mitchell darted back, surprised, but fuelled on by manic desperation Jack barged into him and bundled him on to his back. The two men went down, entangled and making enough noise to turn the deputies away from Emmet.

They rolled away from the tree, but Jack's hand closed on Mitchell's holster and he tore out his gun, then pushed himself away from Mitchell then to his feet.

'Step away from Emmet,' he roared, crouching down.

Mitchell stood, his sneer registering irritation and not concern, but he did gesture down the slope. The deputies splayed out from around Emmet, giving his brother respite, but Emmet stayed slumped against his bonds, oblivious to what Jack was doing.

Jack tore his gaze from Emmet's bloodied form and glanced around, seeing that every lawman stood with a hand dangling close to his holster.

'What you want us to do now?'

Mitchell asked, with only amusement in his tone.

'The situation's changed and I'm in control,' Jack snapped, darting his gun back and forth between the lawmen. 'First, you'll untie Emmet. Then, we're leaving.'

Mitchell snorted. 'You reckon you're a good enough shot to take all six of us on, do you?'

'Perhaps not, but I'll save Emmet or die trying.'

'Only thing you'll do is die.'

Jack glanced around the sprawl of impassive deputies, seeing no sign that any of them would move to release Emmet or that Mitchell was wrong and he'd live for more than a few seconds after he'd fired the first shot.

'But maybe I don't have to shoot you all.' He swung the gun round to aim at Mitchell. 'You'll die first unless you do what I say.'

'I won't.' Mitchell smiled. 'The gun ain't loaded.'

Jack considered Mitchell's calmness

and judged that no matter how many times he'd faced danger, he wouldn't be so cool if the gun *was* loaded.

Jack winced. He'd gambled everything on this last desperate attempt to escape and now it was set to fail before it'd even started.

10

Twenty minutes after Denver, Rico and Deputy Fairborn had separated to scout around, Denver returned to the agreed meeting-place.

He had found no evidence to confirm whether the trail they had been following was Flynn's or whether it was the Turner brothers'. Fairborn was waiting for him, having also failed to learn anything of interest, and while they awaited Rico's return, they debated their next actions.

'We could follow trails for ever and not find Flynn or the gold,' Fairborn said, frowning. 'I reckon we got to do some thinking and piece together what happened back in Broken Rock Canyon.'

Denver considered. 'Flynn tried to steal the gold, but the wagon fell down the side of the canyon. It's a reasonable bet that the Turner brothers got to the wagon first and took the gold.'

'Yeah, but when they reached Bluff Creek they had only one bar on them. So they buried it somewhere between Broken Rock Canyon and town. And as they didn't have much time they wouldn't have left a meandering trail. That means the trail we lost was the Turner brothers' trail, and to find the gold we got to stop following the group that tried to follow them and start thinking like the brothers.'

Denver nodded. He reckoned Flynn's gang had probably made the second trail, but as he had no proof, trying to find the gold felt like a better idea. So, he tried to think from the viewpoint of a bumbling fur-trapper who had happened across a heap of gold.

As he considered, he saw Rico emerge from around the side of a butte, a half-mile away. The sight of this duplicitous man reminded Denver that he was trying to second-guess men who were basically honest. And that meant they would probably act in a straightforward and predictable manner.

'I reckon we keep this simple,' he said. 'We take the most direct route to Bluff Creek from the canyon. Somewhere between here and town, we might find where they buried the gold.'

Fairborn agreed to this plan and joined Denver in watching Rico approach. He sighed.

'I can't believe you trust that Rico.'

Denver laughed. 'Despite what I said earlier, I don't trust anything I've heard from him — not even that he *is* Rico Warren.'

Fairborn shifted round in the saddle to consider Denver.

'What makes you think that?'

'He's wearing a shirt with a bullethole in it, but he ain't injured. He knows more than a lowlife like Rico Warren should know. And he shoots better than I'd expect him to shoot.'

'I guess none of that adds up.' Fairborn whistled under his breath. 'So, who is the man who is calling himself Rico Warren?'

'No idea. But I reckon this man shot the real Rico and for some reason took his shirt. Since then, he's been scheming so much it's almost as if he's been using me to find the gold.'

'And you're letting him think you don't know,' Fairborn mused, a slow smile appearing. 'You figure you can use that to your advantage?'

'Yeah. Sometime soon he'll turn on us. Except he won't expect us to know that he'll do that, and then we can use the distraction.'

Fairborn continued to nod as Rico slowed his horse down and hailed them.

'Have you thought,' he said, lowering his voice, 'that if you're right and this man ain't Rico, he could be a member of Flynn's gang?'

Denver flashed a smile. 'He could even be Flynn himself.'

Fairborn blew out his cheeks. 'A dangerous game, Denver.'

'Aren't they all?'

Denver turned to face Rico and beckoned him to approach. He outlined their plan in which they would stop following trails and take the most direct route to Bluff Creek, attempting to work out which route the Turner brothers would have taken.

Rico offered support for this plan and they headed to a nearby ridge, this being the highest point around from where they could see the surrounding land and choose their route.

They stopped at the crest of the ridge. A lake was ahead with pines coating the slope. Beyond that was patchwork of hogback ridges, buttes and the occasional blind canyon — a route with plenty of choices for men seeking to hide gold.

They looked forward to Bluff Creek, then back to Broken Rock Canyon, and they all agreed that as their current position was on the direct route to Bluff Creek, the brothers had probably headed here. Then they would have headed around the lake, taking the southward route.

Beyond that, they would need to pick up a trail. But as they were confident that they were going in the right direction, they headed down the slope through the trees, taking their time as they searched for tracks. When the brothers had arrived in town it had been the early evening, and that meant they wouldn't have had the time diligently to cover their tracks all the way to town.

And sure enough, when they reached the trees they discovered a trail, and this was quickly joined by another set of tracks.

They stopped to debate what this latest discovery meant. But then a gunshot ripped out, the sound distant, but sounding as if it had come from near the lake.

Denver glanced at Fairborn and Rico, then without further word broke into a gallop.

★　★　★

168

Facing an arc of corrupt lawmen with a gun that might not be loaded, Jack Turner considered the terrible events of the afternoon and recalled an earlier incident.

Mitchell had fired at Emmet on the stake. When he'd ended this display of power, Jack hadn't seen him reload. Mitchell might have done when he wasn't looking, but the sheriff might not be bluffing and the gun could have only one or maybe even no bullets.

Jack firmed his jaw, trying to appear unconcerned by this memory.

'Then throw me your gunbelt,' he demanded.

Mitchell chuckled. 'You know I'm right, don't you? You got yourself an unloaded gun, and now you've had your fun and I can get that gold.'

Mitchell walked towards him with no trace of fear in his steadfast gaze and steady pace.

Jack backed away down the slope. 'Stay away.'

'Not doing that.' Mitchell maintained

his steady pacing. 'You'll give yourself up.'

'I'd sooner die.'

'And you will. But I want to enjoy myself first.'

'I'll shoot you if you don't stop right there.'

Mitchell shrugged, advancing now to within five paces of Jack, who darted his gaze around, seeing that the deputies were edging in too, ready to take him at the first chance they got.

But they moved steadily and didn't rush him — as he would have expected them to do if the gun *was* unloaded.

Jack continued to back away, but turned down the slope to close on Emmet and the deputies. Whether the gun was loaded or not, he reckoned he had enough time to try for one shot before they took him. And that meant he could kill Mitchell, or he could even kill himself.

But a flash of grim understanding came to him and he knew what he had to do.

On flat ground, ten yards before the stake, he stopped.

'Emmet,' he shouted, 'it's time to go.'

Mitchell and his deputies snorted their derision as Emmet raised his bloodied head from the mass of welling blood that was his chest, hope lighting in his eyes despite the circumstances.

Jack locked his eyes on his brother's eyes, conveying a silent plea that he should forgive him, then swung the gun from Mitchell and aimed it at his brother's head.

Emmet didn't flinch away, but maybe the pain had sent him to a place where he wasn't aware of what was happening.

Jack fired, the slug ripping into Emmet's forehead. Then he swung round to face Mitchell and pulled the trigger again. This time his finger twitch produced only a dull click. He fired again and again, but still failed to fire, then hurled the gun at Mitchell and swung round to face the advancing deputies.

He delivered two wild punches that

pummelled the first two deputies who reached him on to their backs. But then they overwhelmed him.

As he collapsed under a mass of bodies, he saw Emmet's dead body standing slumped against his bonds. He consoled himself with the fact that no matter what they did to him now, he had saved his brother from further pain.

Then the bodies lifted from him and Temple stood him straight to face Mitchell.

'He doesn't know what his brother's done with the gold,' Temple said. 'You want us to kill him?'

Mitchell shook his head, a fiendish gleam alighting his eyes.

'No. Keep him alive. He might know something and besides, he's got to suffer for two now.'

★　★　★

Denver, Rico and Fairborn drew their horses to a halt on the edge of the treeline.

Since hearing the gunshot, no further shots had sounded, and now they had found who had fired. Below, Sheriff Mitchell and a group of his deputies were beside the lake.

Mitchell had a wagon upon which a cage stood with a solitary man inside. The group was preparing to move out of their camp. So far, they hadn't acknowledged that they had seen them approaching.

Denver turned to Fairborn, who was already looking at him.

'Reckon we can't avoid this,' Fairborn said. 'We have to see Mitchell.'

'Don't worry about me,' Denver said. 'I guess I have to sort out why this bounty is on my head at some stage.'

Fairborn nodded. Then they both glanced at Rico, but his eyes were glazed and he didn't appear to notice them. Fairborn and Denver both smiled as they set off to ride down into the camp.

Fairborn called on ahead to alert Mitchell and the sheriff swung round to face up the slope. His deputies spread out around him.

As they rode down to the lake, Denver sat tall in the saddle, unconcerned as to what might happen to him. Whatever charges Mitchell felt he should face, he could answer them. His only dubious action had been his decision to keep Rico out of jail, but he felt sure that with Fairborn's help he could explain himself.

Accordingly, he pulled ahead to ride into the camp first, with Rico and Fairborn behind.

'Mitchell,' he said, drawing his horse to a halt, 'I'm Denver Calhoun. I believe you're looking for me.'

A huge smile spread across Mitchell's face. He glanced back at his deputies, receiving a round of nods, then turned back to look at Fairborn.

'Obliged for your help, Deputy,' he said. 'You did a good job in bringing him in.'

'I didn't,' Fairborn reported. 'Denver is here without any encouragement from me. He wants to sort out the charges against him. Then we can all work together to get Flynn and the gold.'

'So,' Mitchell mused, 'you know about the gold.'

'Learnt some interesting things. And I guess you have, too.'

Mitchell nodded then pointed at Rico. 'And who's that with you?'

'Rico Warren.'

Mitchell narrowed his eyes as he peered at Rico, then snorted.

'Of course it is. And why is *Rico* with you?'

'It's a long story and it's one you'll have to consider soon. But for now, just trust me and let's share what we know about Flynn and the gold.'

Mitchell shook his head. 'I want to hear that story now.'

Fairborn shrugged. 'In short — '

'In short,' Rico shouted, prancing his horse forwards to stand beside Denver, 'don't believe anything they say. I'm the one who did what the wanted posters said and brought in Denver Calhoun. And I want my gold bar.'

'Rico!' Fairborn and Denver said together.

'And don't go listening to what they claim,' Rico snapped, waving his arms. 'They got some odd plans in mind. But I played them off against each other and made sure I got to bring Denver in.'

'Be quiet,' Denver muttered. 'I said I'd speak up for you, but I ain't doing that if you don't stop acting like an idiot.'

Rico firmed his jaw. 'You want to listen to the word of a wanted man, Mitchell?'

Denver looked skywards, sighing, but when he lowered his head, he saw that Mitchell was smiling.

'So, you, Rico Warren, are the man who brought in Denver Calhoun,' he said, his gleaming eyes suggesting he found the idea as preposterous as Denver and Fairborn did. 'And you're a bounty hunter now.'

'Sure am,' Rico said, sitting tall.

'Then I guess I got no choice.' Mitchell reached into his pocket. He held his hand inside a moment, looking around and smiling, then withdrew it, but he removed a gold bar. He hefted it, then spun it round and held it out.

Rico sat a moment, his eyebrows raised in surprise, then edged his horse forward. He held his hand out, his slow movements suggesting he still didn't expect his bluff to work. But Mitchell kept his hand firm and let Rico reach down and snatch the bar.

Denver darted a glance at Fairborn, expecting him to protest, but the deputy sat impassive and, with a flash of understanding, Denver ralized what Mitchell was doing. He straightened and watched Rico dart incredulous glances at the various lawmen.

'And I can go now?' he asked.

'Yeah,' Mitchell said, half-turning away. 'I got Denver Calhoun. You got the gold bar. Don't see no reason to keep a busy bounty hunter any longer than I need to.'

Rico backed his horse away, not meeting either Fairborn's or Denver's eyes, but as nobody made a move towards him, he speeded his retreat, then swung his horse around and galloped away from the lake.

Mitchell watched him go, still smiling, and when he disappeared from view into the trees, he snapped quick gestures to a deputy, who hurried to his horse.

'You let him go to follow him,' Denver said.

Fairborn laughed. 'He did. Seems you ain't the only one who does things in unorthodox ways.'

Mitchell nodded. 'Yeah. I don't know who that man is, but he ain't Rico Warren and I reckon he might just lead me to something mighty interesting.'

'Are we all following him?' Fairborn asked.

'No. One man should be enough.'

'Don't underestimate him,' Denver

said. 'He acts like a fool, but it's an act and he's more formidable than he looks.'

'Obliged for the information.' Mitchell barked short orders and another two deputies joined the first in heading out and following Rico. 'And now, I'd like to hear the rest.'

Fairborn nudged his horse forward. 'I'll let Denver explain.'

Mitchell shook his head. 'He won't. First, Denver will surrender his gun and join my other prisoner in the cage. Then you and I will talk.'

Denver opened his mouth to snort his refusal, but Fairborn raised a hand.

'Denver,' he said, 'if you follow orders, it'll be easier for me to sort this out quickly.'

Denver took one last glance at Mitchell, then his remaining deputies and their matching cold gazes suggested that the lawmen would listen only to a fellow lawman. Denver dismounted, handed over his gun, and joined the other prisoner in the mobile cell on the wagon.

As Fairborn and Mitchell headed off to stand beside the camp's dying fire and talk, Denver sat and considered his fellow prisoner. And he now recognized him as one of the men he'd helped in Bluff Creek.

That man sat morose and subdued in a corner of the cage, not even looking up to register Denver's arrival.

'You Jack Turner?' Denver asked.

The man didn't reply immediately, staying hunched and staring at the floor of the cell, but slowly he raised his head to look at Denver. The eyes were dull and perhaps unfocused, as he failed to meet Denver's eyes.

'Yeah,' he murmured, his voice low and defeated. He slowly ran his gaze up to Denver's face. His eyes flashed as he registered his identity. Then he returned to staring at the floor. 'You probably saved my life back in Bluff Creek.'

'Then you ought to be looking more pleased.'

Jack snorted. 'What have I got to be pleased about?'

'Plenty, if you're innocent.'

'I am innocent and right now that's the worse thing about all this.'

'What you mean?'

Jack looked up and fixed Denver with his watery gaze.

'I mean handing yourself over to Sheriff Mitchell was the biggest mistake of your life. And it was your last.'

'I trust the law.'

'And I used to, too. But Sheriff Mitchell ain't like any lawman I've ever met.' Jack glanced out through the bars at the lawmen. Fairborn and Mitchell were talking by the fire, but behind the deputy, Mitchell's two other deputies were moving in towards him. 'And neither you nor me will leave here alive.'

11

'I don't believe you,' Denver said. 'Deputy Fairborn is a decent lawman and — '

'And perhaps he is, but Mitchell ain't.' Jack pointed through the cell bars at Fairborn, who was gesturing around him as he explained what he knew to Mitchell.

'Prove it.'

Jack shuffled along the bottom of the cell and drew Denver's attention to a tangle of logs beside the lake.

'Mitchell tied my brother to one of those logs and his deputies tortured him until . . . until he died. Then they threw his body into the lake.' He gulped. 'He died before they'd learned what he'd done with the gold and that's the only reason I'm still alive — for now.'

'And do you know where the gold is?'

Denver asked, although he still didn't believe Jack's story.

'I got an idea now.' Jack shrugged. 'Won't do me no good.'

Jack lowered his head and, as he didn't appear ready to volunteer anything more, Denver stood and peered through the cell bars. With his eyes narrowed, he saw blood on the ground between two of the logs.

Then he saw a bloodied knife lying on the nearest log. And when he saw a loop of rope lying around the base of another log, as if it'd been used to tie someone up, he started thinking that Jack was right and that he'd made a terrible mistake.

When he saw that the end of the log was dirty as if it had been driven into the ground, he accepted that Jack had told him the truth and that he had walked into hell.

He rocked from side to side, trying to draw Fairborn's attention without any of the other lawmen noticing him, but Fairborn was standing sideways to him and Denver wasn't in his eyeline. But Mitchell was and he flinched, then looked at the cell.

Mitchell and Denver locked gazes. Mitchell's eyes opened wide, his sudden action stating that he was aware that Denver now knew the truth of what was happening here.

With no time left to warn Fairborn surreptitiously, Denver grabbed the bars and shook them.

'Fairborn,' he yelled, 'watch out!'

Fairborn swung round, staring in all directions as he searched for the danger that had shocked Denver, but the danger was far closer than he could possibly imagine.

Mitchell waited until Fairborn had his back to him, then drew his gun and crashed it down on the back of his head, pole-axing him. Then he shouted orders to his deputies and these men moved in towards the cell.

Denver glared at Fairborn's supine body, willing him to rise, but then accepted he would get no help there.

He turned to watch the deputies halt before the wagon.

Mitchell jumped on to the back of the wagon. He waited until the other two deputies joined him, then unlocked the door.

'Get him out here,' Mitchell snarled. 'It's time to find out what he knows.'

While Mitchell stood to the side, his deputies paced into the cell.

One of them clutched a length of chain behind his back. The other brandished a short iron bar. But Denver stood in the centre of the cell and kept his stance casual. Behind him, Jack shuffled backwards to cower into the far corner.

'You want me out there,' Denver said, rolling his shoulders, 'you got to come get me.'

The deputy clutching the chain glanced over his shoulder at Mitchell and received a nod, but Denver didn't let him carry out his order and charged him. He hit the deputy full in the side and carried him on into the bars.

Mitchell barked orders outside the cell, but Denver blotted them from his mind as he grabbed the deputy's collar. The other deputy leapt on his back and looped the bar around his neck, then tugged backwards, but Denver concentrated on incapacitating the man in his grip.

He slammed him into the bars, then again a second time, the blow smashing his head with a dull clang. The deputy went limp but Denver knocked him into the bars a third time then lunged for the chain, tearing it from his grasp as he fell.

He swung the chain back over his shoulder, but couldn't get enough leverage to hit the man holding with him any force, and the two men scraped and shuffled round on the spot.

But the deputy had such a firm grip of his neck that motes of darkness sprinkled themselves across Denver's vision — he had to fight his way out of this headlock within seconds or he'd lose consciousness through lack of air.

Through his pained vision, he saw that Mitchell had paced into the cell doorway, his gun drawn and aimed at the struggling twosome, his weapon being the only gun in sight. Denver fought his way around to turn his back on Mitchell then strode a shuffling pace towards the back wall.

The deputy resisted, pulling himself away from Denver and, with a gap opening up between them, Denver played out the bunched chain to its utmost then swung it over his shoulder.

The deputy grunted. Denver reckoned he'd been lucky and delivered a solid blow to his head. He pulled down, but even though the chain only moved a few inches, Denver used enough force to slam the man into his back, knocking them both into the cell wall.

Denver realized that he'd looped the chain around the deputy's neck and, taking advantage of his luck, ran his hand up the chain, tightening it, then yanked downwards.

He couldn't secure a grip that was as

tight as the grip the man had gained around his throat, but he did drag the deputy's head over his shoulder and crunch his forehead into the cell bars. Then he knocked him into the bars a second time.

The arm holding the bar against his throat relaxed its grip, letting Denver drag in a breath and, with a burst of strength, he threw all his energy into dropping to his knees and yanking hard on the chain. The deputy lunged forward, his feet leaving the floor as he slammed into the wall with solid force, freeing his grip of Denver's neck.

Denver surged to his feet, swinging round. He heard Mitchell shouting out a warning, but he put that from his mind. He hurled back his arm, then delivered a sharp upper cut to the deputy's chin that cracked his head back. And a second round-armed slug wheeled him to the floor, where he slid across the cell before folding into a hunched pile in the corner.

Then Denver swirled around. The

echoing blast of a gunshot accompanied his movement. Denver winced but then saw that the shot had been high and involuntary. Mitchell had slipped into the cell to get a better angle on Denver, but he had ignored the seemingly irrelevant menace of Jack, and that had let Jack roll to his feet and grab him.

Mitchell held Jack at arm's length and would free himself within seconds, but that was all the time Denver needed. He strode three long paces then slugged Mitchell's jaw. Mitchell stumbled away from Jack's grip and shrugged off the blow, but he didn't regain his wits fast enough and Denver followed through with a flurry of blows that pummelled him one way then the other.

A whirling upper cut to the chin crashed his head into the bars and he slid down them, to lie with his legs splayed and his head lolling.

Denver confirmed that the sheriff was out cold while Jack gathered his gun. Then Denver hurried over to one of the other unconscious deputies. He secured a gun, then turned to see that Jack was standing over Mitchell's body, Mitchell's gun clutched in two shaking hands and aimed down at him.

'Jack,' Denver urged, 'Mitchell may have killed your brother and he may be an evil critter, but that don't give you the right to kill a lawman in cold blood.'

Jack snorted, the tremor in his hands suggesting he'd ignore Denver's plea, but then he swung round and stamped a foot on the floor.

'I guess you're right,' he said. He paced over Mitchell's body, but then stopped and swung round to crunch a solid kick into Mitchell's ribs. 'But I reckon I feel better after that.'

Denver conceded that and he hurried past Jack to the door, but then lead cannoned into the cell bars, took a ricochet, and whistled across the cell. Denver darted his head around, searching for which of the deputies had come to, but then saw that the danger didn't come from within the cell, it came from outside.

Deputy Temple Kelly and the other deputies had returned.

Denver moved to get out of the cell, but a volley of slugs tore into the cell door, the bullets whistling and whining in all directions and forcing him to dive to the floor. On his belly, he joined Jack.

The sides of the wagon ensured he couldn't see much of the surrounding landscape, or the deputies, but it also provided him with cover. But sitting proud and high in a metal cell, that cover didn't fill Denver with any confidence.

He patted Jack's back and smiled, hoping to see the same level of confidence he'd seen in Rico when they'd been attacked in Broken Rock Canyon, but now that he'd defeated Mitchell, Jack looked back without hope in his dull eyes.

Denver judged that he'd been through far too much already. To get out of this situation he needed to act on his own.

'Hey,' he shouted, raising his head slightly, 'how's Rico?'

'Couldn't find him,' Temple shouted from nearby, perhaps twenty yards from the wagon. 'So we came back for you.'

'You won't get me. I'm holding Mitchell hostage in here.'

'You got nothing.'

Denver glanced at Mitchell, but accepted that when faced with men as ruthless as these were, using him to escape was doomed to fail. He needed to get away from the cell and gain a better position. He whispered quick orders to Jack to stay where he was and to take out any target that presented itself.

Jack returned a murmur and a shrug and, accepting that that was the most encouragement he'd get, Denver crawled across the cell and out through the door. On his belly, he snaked to the end of the wagon. The view beyond the wagon slowly opened up to him, but with the wagon turned towards the lake and the small promontory of land, he didn't see any of the deputies.

He decided to slip to the ground and take up a position beneath the wagon, but then something jabbed up into his belly. He flinched, raising himself slightly, then winced.

A rifle barrel was poking up through the gap between two boards. And his guts were the target.

'Move an inch,' a voice ordered from beneath the wagon, 'and I'll rip you in two.'

12

With a rifle jabbed into his belly, Denver saw no choice but to drop his gun over the side of the wagon, then stay precisely where he was. He hoped that maybe Jack would help him, but when Temple and the other deputies moved into view, Jack instantly dropped his gun without putting up a fight.

Within five minutes, Denver, Jack and the now semi-conscious Deputy Fairborn sat in a huddle with guns trained down on them while Temple set about rousing the others.

And when Mitchell came to and learned that Temple had lost Rico's trail, his flaring eyes and determined pace as he walked towards them showed he was now in the mood to take out his anger on someone.

He pushed the deputies who were guarding his prisoners aside and loomed over them. He rubbed his ribs, darting his glance at each man in turn, his grin suggesting that he was choosing which one of them would die first. His gaze stopped at Denver.

'Stake him out on the ground,' he said, gesturing to Temple. 'I want to see how tough this one really is.'

Denver tensed himself, ready to jump to his feet and die in a futile attempt to escape rather than have Mitchell tear him apart, but Jack raised his head.

'Wait,' he said, his quiet voice carrying enough assurance to halt the lawmen.

'Why?' Mitchell asked.

Jack rubbed his forehead, wincing as if he was suffering more than just physical pain.

'You only killed Emmet because you want the gold. And I'm the only one who knows where Emmet hid it. Don't make anybody else suffer.'

'Then talk. Now.'

Jack nodded towards the tangle of logs beside the lake.

'I'll show you.' He stood and slowly paced towards the logs.

Nobody moved to stop him and he hunkered down beside one of the logs, then paced over it to consider the second log. He bent and when he stood and turned, he was clutching a short length of rope, which he tugged, confirming that one end was still under the first log. He smiled as if this discovery proved where the gold was.

Mitchell cocked his head to one side.

'What you trying to tell me?' he asked.

'Emmet tied these logs together.'

'Perhaps he did,' Mitchell said, 'but that don't answer my question. What did he do with the gold?'

Jack slumped down on the log and rested his elbows on his knees as he stared at the ground. He sighed then looked up at Mitchell, smiling, although after all the terrible things that had happened to him, his blank eyes provided no suggestion of humour.

'Emmet had an axe,' he reported,

slapping the wood at his side. 'And he chopped these here logs down, then lashed them together.'

Mitchell nodded and turned round to look up into the forest.

'Then we just got to find the stumps of the trees he chopped down and the gold will be buried there.'

Jack shook his head. 'That won't help.'

Mitchell swirled round to confront Jack.

'What you mean?'

Jack looked at the forest then looked over his shoulder at the lake.

'I mean you're looking in the wrong direction,' he said.

★   ★   ★

With the logs Emmet had been pulling apart when Mitchell had come upon him lashed together again, Jack, Denver and Fairborn paddled out on to the lake.

Denver sat at one end of their

makeshift raft, pushing them through the water with a short bough, while Fairborn paddled at the front and Jack directed them from the centre. Twenty yards from the side, Denver detected a current that ran sideways and rippled the water, and which forced them to paddle at an angle to continue travelling in the direction Jack had indicated. Otherwise the lake was placid.

Mitchell had believed Jack's story. He had placed their belongings, including their guns, in a pile at the bottom of the slope. Then he had set his prisoners to work on retrieving the gold from Emmet's hiding-place. Mitchell was unconcerned that letting them row out on to the lake would give them a chance to escape, as out there they were sitting targets for the deputies who spread out along the promontory.

'All right,' Fairborn whispered when they had rowed far enough to be out of the lawmen's earshot, 'I'm familiar with the double-bluff, but what do we do now?'

'That was no bluff,' Jack said.

Denver and Fairborn both snorted.

'No need to keep up the pretence. Mitchell only just believed you when you said Emmet had dropped the gold into the lake, but he had to accept your word. And none of us believed Mitchell when he said he'd let us live if we found the gold.'

'You're right about the last bit, but I wasn't bluffing when I said this is where I reckon Emmet hid the gold.'

Fairborn glanced at Denver. 'What you think?'

'I reckon,' Denver said, 'that our only hope is to play along and search for the gold. If we're lucky, a chance will come to do something, and when it does, we got to take it.'

Fairborn nodded and Denver returned to looking at the lake, but the water was too murky for him to see what was below them and the lake itself was featureless, without islands to break the still waters.

But Jack had a confident set to his

jaw and he directed them on with frequent glances at the promontory of land that pointed out into the water towards them. Once they were level with the tip of the promontory, he called for them to stop. With his arms outstretched to maintain his balance he stood, looked around, then sat.

'This is it,' he declared.

'This is it,' Denver and Fairborn murmured together then looked at each other to snort their scepticism.

'Yeah,' Jack said, his voice sounding hurt. 'We often fished here. It's far enough away from the — '

'Spare us the explanations,' Fairborn said. 'This location has to be a guess and you know it.'

'This location has to be right,' Jack declared. 'Emmet may have acted stupidly, but he had plenty of sense usually. He took one gold bar and buried the rest, but anywhere where he buried it could get found and the gold dug up, except here. Nobody would ever guess the gold would be in the lake, except him. And now me.'

'And how do you expect us to get the gold? Fish for it?'

'No.' Jack placed his hands together and mimed diving into the water.

Fairborn shook his head and glanced at Denver for support. Although Denver held out little hope that they would find the gold here, he accepted that arguing about whether or not the gold was at the bottom of the lake was getting them nowhere.

So, after shouting to Mitchell about what they planned to do, he rolled off the log raft and into the water. He treaded water as he took deep breaths, then dived, swimming straight down.

The water was so murky he could see only a few feet ahead of him and the light level dropped rapidly. And it was with a start that he reached the bottom, only seeing it as block of darkness ahead before his outstretched hands touched it. He drove down once more, temporarily managing to float just above the bottom.

Then he swam around on the spot, seeing nothing but a few square feet of the silt-filled lake bottom. He swam in a short circle, fighting to stay near the bottom, but his need for air twitched in his lungs.

He thrust down then kicked off from the bottom, reaching the surface in two long thrusts of his arms and legs. He threw back his head, freeing water from his hair, then shook his head.

'This *is* impossible,' he reported. 'The water's too murky. You could be a foot from the gold and still not see it.'

'If we give up, Mitchell will kill us,' Jack said.

'Then jump in and help,' Denver said. 'Or we'll never find it.'

'I can't swim,' Jack said.

'I guess I can,' Fairborn murmured, with a resigned sigh and a glance at the impatient lawmen parading on the promontory. 'But that don't change the fact that this could take hours, perhaps days, perhaps for ever. And Mitchell won't like that.'

Denver agreed with this gloomy prognosis and, after glancing at the vast expanse of water around them, Jack even mustered a slow nod.

But despite everyone's pessimism, two hours later they located the gold.

Fairborn had provided several good ideas to aid their search, including dropping ropes weighted down with rocks into the water to let the diver orient himself when underwater.

Denver didn't mind this approach — the more complex the operation, the more time for the lawmen to relax, and the more time it bought them to await a potential distraction.

When they'd searched the immediate area they released the rocks to give them a clue as to the area they'd already searched. Denver and Fairborn continued to take turns to dive, and when Fairborn burst up from the water, grinning and pointing downwards they were just a dozen yards from the position Jack had directed them to in the first place.

With the box located, Fairborn secured it with a rope, but when they tried to drag it up from the lake bottom, their straining almost capsized the raft. So Denver ordered them to bring the bars up individually.

Fairborn dived and broke the surface holding a gold bar in each hand. Then Denver followed and emerged with three, one in each hand and another pressed to his chest. But Fairborn earned a laugh from the other two men when he dived and emerged with six bars piled high against his chest and one clutched under his chin. Although when he admitted he had dropped one on the way up, Denver shouted orders to them to limit themselves to bringing up two bars at a time, one in each hand.

As the day wore on, the pile of bars on the raft grew dangerously high, but Denver didn't want them to head to land and so risk not being able to locate the box again. So, they continued to dive, and Denver continued to run his gaze along the side of the lake, hanging on to the small hope that maybe Rico would return and give them a distraction.

In the short periods between placing the gold bars on the raft and the next man diving, Denver and Fairborn exchanged brief and muttered plans.

None of them believed that Mitchell would let them live once they'd fulfilled their purpose, but neither could they devise a plan that wouldn't get them killed the moment they tried it.

The only real hope was to head away from the lakeside. But they were forty yards from dry land, which was near enough to ensure that if they tried to swim or row to safety, the lawmen were sure to shoot them before they'd gone too far. But Denver reckoned that if a better idea didn't come to him soon, he'd take that chance.

They had just six bars left to claim when Fairborn surfaced and offered a desperate suggestion.

'The water's right murky,' he said to

Denver as he slowly placed the bars on the raft.

'Yeah?' Denver said.

'You can't see more than a few feet under water.'

Denver furrowed his brow but as asking for more details would appear suspicious to the men watching on dry land, he dived to the bottom. He collected two bars, leaving just four, but still couldn't see why the fact that the water was murky had encouraged Fairborn.

But when he kicked off to head back to the raft, he noted that despite the bright light from above, he had to swim to within two strokes of the surface before he even saw the raft.

He gathered his breath as he slammed the bars on the raft.

'Understood,' he said, 'when we going for it?'

'Next time,' Fairborn said, then dived.

'Don't know what you're planning,' Jack whispered on the raft while still keeping his gaze placid and directed at the shore. 'But what do you want me to do?'

'You can't do much but start praying when the shooting starts.'

'Got to be able to do more than that. This gold killed both my brothers. I guess I'd sooner die out here trying something, however desperate, than just hand it over to Mitchell.'

Denver nodded. He would have tipped all the gold over the side in a final act of defiance if he thought it wouldn't take Mitchell long to reclaim it.

'When Fairborn comes up, we're both diving together. Count to thirty. Then we need a distraction. I guess paddling away as fast as you can is sure to get Mitchell's attention, and sure to get you . . . '

Denver sighed then flashed Jack an encouraging smile, receiving a forlorn one in return. Then he devoted himself to breathing deeply until Fairborn surfaced.

And when the lawman appeared, he burst clear of the water some five yards ahead of the raft, glanced around then waved at Mitchell.

'I found something,' he shouted.

'What is it?' Mitchell said, coming to the edge of the water.

Fairborn swam to the side of the raft and slapped the two gold bars he'd collected on it, then turned.

'More gold I reckon.' He glanced back. 'Denver, check it out with me.'

He dived. Mitchell shouted out, ordering Denver to ignore that instruction, but by then Denver was already diving, cutting off the end of the order.

For two strokes, he pushed himself down, then levelled off and aimed for the lakeside. Denver had never tried to swim so far underwater and he had no idea whether he could reach the land before his lungs gave out.

But he had to try.

Below the surface he could neither see nor hear what was happening above water. He could only hear the water rushing by and he peered ahead, hoping to see Fairborn, but the murk that would stop Mitchell seeing what they were doing under water also ensured that he couldn't see him.

After a dozen strokes his lungs screeched out for air, but he drove on, staying just beneath the surface. Then the lightness above and the dark bottom of the lake below closed on him as Denver swam to the edge of the lake.

He kept the land to his side as he swam along the side of the promontory, making sure that he got as far along it as he possibly could before he had to break the surface. Blood pounded in his ears, the pressure was bursting his lungs, and he finally had to admit defeat. He had to breathe or die.

He thrust sideways, his feet pushing off from the bottom and he broke the surface with far less grace than he would have hoped.

But he needn't have worried about attracting attention because Mitchell and his deputies already knew what they were doing. Two men stood on the edge of the promontory shouting orders to Jack, who was paddling desperately, but had managed to get only a few yards further away. The other deputies had lined up and were firing down into the water twenty yards to Denver's side, presumably guessing their positions.

'They're there,' one man shouted, swirling round to face Denver.

'That's only Denver,' another shouted, but Denver didn't wait around and he dragged in a deep breath, then dived.

The water was only shoulder-deep. He crouched down on the bottom of the water, then kicked off from the bottom, aiming for deeper water.

He presumed that the lawmen were firing down into the water at him, but the blanket of water ensured he couldn't see any sign of them doing that. He glimpsed a shape ahead before it moved out of view. Denver followed it, catching fleeting glimpses of Fairborn's trailing feet, but the deputy was a better swimmer than Denver was and he quickly moved out of view.

Denver swam after him, but then saw that ahead the bottom was again rising. Unable to get his bearings, Denver veered off to the side, but again the land rose before him. He accepted that he'd come to the end of the promontory and had now reached a point where the land was around him on most sides.

He debated trying to find deeper water so that he could evade the lawmen before coming to the surface some distance away, but his lungs were screaming for air again and he let himself rise to the surface.

He emerged gently, but the scene he faced was far from serene.

Ten yards to his side, Fairborn and one of the deputies were struggling in the shallows, and the other deputies were congregating on the side, covering them.

Denver ducked down below the water, unsure as to whether they'd seen him, then pushed on. He managed two strokes before the water became so shallow he had to emerge. So, he surged from the water, the shallows waist-deep, and waded towards dry ground, ignoring the deputies' shouts further along the promontory.

He had one destination in mind — the small site where Mitchell had piled their belongings. He had to hope that Mitchell had been too confident to bother securing their guns.

He waded out of the water then broke into a run.

Mitchell shouted out for Temple to shoot him, but Denver thrust his head down and ran. Mitchell had thrown their baggage inside a small circle of saddles some thirty yards ahead at the bottom of the slope and he ignored everything but covering that distance as quickly as he could.

He heard Temple running after him and lead tore at his heels, whistling the grit into his wet calves, but he sprinted the last few yards, then threw himself over the nearest saddle. He rolled over a shoulder and slammed to a halt on his side, then scrambled round on his belly to rummage beneath their baggage.

His hands closed on air.

The guns weren't there.

He hurled baggage around and thrust his hands beneath the saddles, but Mitchell had taken the guns, after all. He ventured a glance up to see that only Temple had followed him; the others were covering Fairborn's fight in the shallows.

Lead tore into leather, forcing Denver to duck.

He had just seconds before Temple got an angle on him and could see him. He scrambled around, looking for something with which to defend himself, but then his hand closed on a short iron bar. It was the bar the deputy had held when he'd tried to beat Denver in the cell, and one end of the bar was sharp. He palmed it, then listened to Temple's approaching footsteps, judging his exact position.

Then he flung back his arm and

surged to his feet, dancing to the side.

Temple had enough time for one shot which tore through a trailing end of Denver's jacket, inches from his chest. But then Denver hurled the bar, the sharp end catching the light of the lowering sun as it hurtled through the air and scythed into Temple's neck. Temple threw his hands to his neck, his fingers clawing at the redness flooding around the bar, as Denver vaulted the saddles and ran towards him.

He reached him, wrestled his gun from Temple's dying grasp, then hunkered down.

Fairborn chose that moment to end his fight in the shallows with a huge slug to his opponent's chin, the blow hammering the deputy into deeper water. But the deputies on dry land spread out and demanded that he raise his hands.

Denver fired at them, his first shot being wild, but forcing them to duck and swirl round.

Fairborn took his chance, running at the deputies as Denver fired again, this time hammering lead into a deputy's side and knocking him into the water.

Caught in a moment of indecision, the other deputies glanced back and forth, giving Denver enough time to hit one full in the chest, then jump to his feet and run towards them.

Mitchell hurried along the side of the promontory, as Denver peppered lead across the other deputies. His deadly aim whirled the first man round to lie face down in the water and took the last one as he emerged from the water.

And when his gunshot echoes faded, that left just Sheriff Mitchell. But Denver had to throw open the chamber to punch in another bullet, and that gave Mitchell enough time to take careful aim.

Fairborn was twenty yards from Denver and unable to help him. Denver threw himself to the ground, rolling to escape from the sheriff's gunfire. Then it came, a huge explosion ripping out, but none of that lead came Denver's way and when he rolled to a halt on his belly and looked up, he saw that Mitchell was on the receiving end.

The corrupt lawman spun round on the spot, his limbs wheeling in a final crazy dance of death with redness exploding from his chest, before he went down, holed repeatedly.

Denver glanced at Fairborn, but he was shaking his head and looking over Denver's shoulder.

Denver winced, then rolled round to look behind him. From out of the trees six men emerged, walking slowly with guns drawn and smoking. With each steady pace, the men thundered lead into the bodies of the deputies, ensuring they were dead.

Denver had seen only one of the men before, but he was sure who the rest were.

'Rico,' he said, 'I guess you've just saved my life again.'

The leading man, Rico, paced to a halt before Denver and beamed a huge smile.

'I have,' he said, 'but now that this is over, you can call me Flynn.'

13

The Flynn gang lined up by the side of the lake.

With six men facing him, Denver had no choice but to drop his unloaded gun at his feet and, while two of the Flynn gang covered him and Fairborn, the others headed to the end of the promontory.

One man stood on the edge and called out to Jack.

'We got your friends here,' he shouted. 'If you want them to live, bring the gold back to land.'

Out on the water, Jack lowered his head a moment, but as he'd managed to paddle only a dozen yards and Fairborn and Denver's escape attempt had now ended, he shrugged, then paddled the raft back to land.

Fairborn leaned in towards Denver to whisper to him.

'Rico . . . Flynn . . . whoever he is ain't letting us live.'

'No argument there,' Denver whispered back. 'But he's saved my life twice now and that means he thinks too much. We still might get a distraction. Watch for it.'

Fairborn nodded slowly and stood tall.

Out on the lake, Jack paddled furiously but it still took him several minutes to reach shallow water, at which stage Flynn gestured for two of his men to wade in and drag the gold-laden raft on to dry land.

With the raft moored but with half its length floating, the outlaws tried to drag it ashore, but the gold teetered dangerously and so Flynn ordered Jack to unload it.

Jack rolled off the raft and into the shallow water. He unloaded two gold bars and threw them ashore, then another two. Denver judged that Jack was working slowly to delay the inevitable end once he'd unloaded the gold. To hurry him on Flynn ordered Fairborn and Denver to help him.

Denver and Fairborn stood beside one end of the raft and Jack stood at the other end. Still working steadily, they hurled the gold on to the shore.

While they worked one of the outlaws manoeuvred Sheriff Mitchell's wagon so that it stood beside the water. Then the six outlaws stood in a line watching the heap of gold grow with grins consuming their faces.

Each time Denver threw another bar on to dry land he glanced at the outlaws, attempting to judge what their weaknesses might be. The lure of the gold had been enticing enough to get numerous men killed over the last few days. But Denver had little time to sow any seeds of disharmony amongst them.

He shuffled round to face the man he'd known as Rico.

'So,' he said while he worked, 'you're not Rico Warren?'

'My first name is Rico, but I'm not Rico Warren.'

'But you are Flynn . . . Rico Flynn, the leader of this gang?'

'Yeah, but then again, nope.' Rico chuckled, then pointed along the line of outlaws. 'I'm Flynn, but so is he, and so is he, and so is all of us.'

Denver straightened up and nodded. 'You're brothers?'

'Yup. We don't have no leader. That's why we're so successful. Everyone has been searching for one leader, but not six equals, all working together like only brothers can.'

As Jack snorted, Denver bent to grab the last handful of gold. He hadn't known that the Flynn gang were brothers and he wondered if this was the moment when someone would decide to shoot them, but Rico only ordered them to load the gold on to the wagon.

'And why were you claiming to be Rico Warren?'

'The best way of keeping away from trouble is to not look like trouble in the first place. It's worked so far for me.'

Rico pointed at the gold. 'And now it's worked very well.'

'And what you planning to do with this much gold?'

'That's no concern of yours.'

'Just wondering.' Denver waded out of the water. 'There's plenty of gold here, but who gets the biggest cut amongst men who are all equal?'

As Denver stomped his feet on dry land, freeing a flood of water, he darted his gaze around, searching for any possibility that this family would self-destruct in a squabble over the gold. But he detected only eager anticipation of making off with it together.

'What you mean?' Rico snapped, narrowing his eyes.

'I mean that plenty of men have died trying to get hold of this gold. I just wonder if — '

'You just wonder if the same will happen to us.' Rico snorted. 'It won't. We're brothers and brothers don't argue over things like gold.'

Fairborn and Denver grabbed the nearest gold bars as they prepared to follow Rico's orders, but Jack stood still in the water, his eyes wild and his breath snorting through his nostrils.

'We're brothers,' he intoned, speaking slowly. 'And brothers don't argue over things like gold.'

'They don't,' Rico said, turning his gaze on Jack.

'They don't!' Jack roared, his face now bright red. 'They don't. They just don't. But they do!'

'Jack,' Fairborn urged, 'load the gold on the wagon and stop ranting.'

But Jack was past listening to sense as he stormed on to dry land to face up to the Flynn gang and their line of drawn guns.

'I ain't doing nothing I don't want to,' he shouted, even stamping his feet for emphasis.

'You will,' Rico muttered, raising his gun and sighting Jack's chest.

'Not any more I don't because you're wrong. Brothers do argue and I lost two brothers over this . . . over this . . . over this heap of nothing.' Jack threw back his head and roared with frustration, then dropped to his knees and grabbed a gold bar. 'I have had enough of this. This gold just makes men lie and cheat and argue and kill each other. And it ain't worth it.'

Jack swirled round, looking as if he was about to hurl the gold bar into the lake. But when he released the bar, he threw it at the nearest outlaw, who ducked. He didn't move fast enough and the bar sliced a glancing blow off his forehead, knocking him to his knees.

The gold bar scooted away along the shoreline as Jack grabbed another bar and advanced on the outlaw with it raised above his head.

The other Flynn brothers glanced at each other. Two men shouted taunts at the injured brother. The others either smiled or furrowed their brows, perhaps Jack's revelation was distracting them for a moment, but none of them moved as Jack advanced on the injured man then swung the gold around as though it was a knife. The outlaw rolled back on his haunches and evaded the swinging bar, but Denver and Fairborn simultaneously judged that this distraction would be the best chance they'd get. They moved for the only weapons open to them — the gold bars.

They knelt and grabbed two bars apiece, but their movements caught the attention of the nearest outlaw who swung round to face them. A command that they stand back half-emerged, but then died on his lips as Denver hurled his bars, the gold smashing into the outlaw's face and snapping his head back.

The outlaw fell into the wagon as Fairborn launched the other two gold bars at Rico and another outlaw. Both bars missed, but his targets ducked and that gave Denver enough time to take three long paces and loom over the outlaw he'd hit.

The man was arched back over the wagon and Denver delivered a back-handed swipe to his cheek that rolled him along the side of the wagon. With his other hand he lunged for his gun.

The weapon came to hand and Denver swirled round with the gun brandished. In front of him Jack and his assailant were tussling, both men clutching the gold bar high above their heads. And Fairborn had grabbed another two bars to hurl at the nearest outlaws.

But Jack's sudden act of pure madness had bought them all the time it could and the Flynn gang tore lead into Fairborn's chest from two different directions, the bullets spinning him around and to the ground.

Denver hunched and his gun spewed lead in three crisp and deadly shots. His first two shots took the outlaws who had shot Fairborn, and he aimed the third at Rico, but Rico dived for cover behind the wagon.

Denver dropped to one knee, the action saving him from a slug that tore into the wood above his head. Taking careful aim, he hammered repeated gunfire into the shooter. The lead knocked the man upright before he tumbled backwards into the water.

And that left just Rico, another outlaw, and another fighting with Jack. He watched the two men rolling over each other, each trying to pummel the other with the gold bar, as he reloaded. Then he dropped to his belly and rolled beneath the wagon to emerge on the other side, but when he peered out, none of the Flynn gang was on the other side.

He narrowed his eyes as he darted his gaze around, but then lead ripped into the dirt beside him. He rolled away and, on his back, fired upwards, peppering his gunfire through the wooden base of the wagon.

As he reloaded he listened and looked up through the gaps in the wooden base, but couldn't see either of the men who must have jumped on the wagon. He'd splayed gunfire wildly and, with luck, should have hit someone.

But then he noticed that he couldn't see through all the gaps between the planks. Metal reinforced one end of the wagon where the mobile cell stood, and as he couldn't see anyone through the gaps in the wood, Rico and the other man must be standing there.

And the moment he emerged from under the wagon in any direction, they'd see him.

Denver waited, hoping that maybe his silence and Rico's frayed nerves would make him think they'd hit him with a lucky shot.

Beyond the wagon Jack was still fighting, his body too close to his assailant for the outlaws on the wagon to shoot him, but they were weakening and soon one of them would wrestle himself clear of the other man.

Denver couldn't wait much longer before making his move and he was debating when to act when a boot edged down on his side of the wagon.

Denver had become used to Rico's sneaky behaviour and, as the boot hung there slackly, he didn't reckon a foot was in it, but neither did it look as if there was a gun in it.

He peered at the boot, still being cautious enough to keep away from the toe end, but then winced and dropped, the action saving him from a bullet that tore out from the opposite direction. The boot had been a distraction, and one of Rico's typical acts.

As he lay on his back he saw a gun swing round beneath the wagon, firing blind and wildly. Denver rolled away, the undirected gunfire kicking up dirt beneath the wagon as he rolled clear.

The other outlaw was edging over the side to get a drop on him, too, and Denver fired up, his shot neatly puncturing the outlaw through the forehead and snapping his head back. Denver rolled once more to get fully clear of the wagon, then jumped to his feet.

He vaulted on to the wagon to face Rico, who was snapping round to face him. His gun arced round to aim at

Denver, but Denver didn't give Rico time to fire and hammered a slug into his side that sent him sprawling over the side of the wagon.

Then Denver followed through, running over the wagon to peer over the other side.

Rico wasn't there.

He darted his gaze up and was just in time to see Rico roll behind the heap of gold. Now he had him pinned down and Denver stood with his legs planted wide as he waited for the moment he showed himself.

'I guess Jack was right,' Denver taunted. 'Even brothers are destined to die over that gold.'

'We weren't fighting each other,' Rico snapped. 'And you won't get it.'

'You're right. But I don't want it.' Denver chuckled. 'And that's why I'll live and you'll die.'

'You're wrong,' Rico roared and leapt up to stand upright, his gun swirling in towards Denver, but Denver had already aimed. He fired.

Denver's deadly shot through the chest staggered Rico back a pace but, with the grim determination that had driven so many men on in their desperate desire to get the gold, he righted himself and paced forward. Denver fired again, tearing a shot through his shoulder.

Still, Rico paced again, struggling to raise his gun, but a final shot to the neck spun him round to lie sprawled over the gold pile, the bars parting to let his face bury itself in the gold.

Denver watched Rico's chest rise and fall as he breathed his last, then turned to look at the last fight, but now Jack had knocked his assailant on his back.

And he was pummelling the supine man with a gold bar.

From the thick blood pooling around the outlaw's head, Denver reckoned the man was dead already and he jumped down from the wagon to stand behind Jack.

He waited until Jack swung the gold bar upwards, then grabbed the bar and stopped him swinging it down again.

'That's enough,' he said. 'You've already ended this.'

Jack tore the bar from Denver's grasp and dashed the outlaw's head. Again, he raised the bar.

'I ain't. I can never end this.' Jack punctuated each comment with another dash of the bar. 'This is for Emmet. And this is for Horace. And this is for every damn fool man that died over this useless gold. This is all it gets you.' He slammed the gold bar down one last time on to the mashed head of the last man to die trying to get the gold, then hurled the bar into the water to kneel hunched and breathing deeply. 'This is all it gets you.'

Denver patted Jack's shoulder. He roved his gaze over Rico and his outlaw brothers, then at Mitchell's corrupt lawmen before it finally centred on Deputy Fairborn.

'Yeah,' he said. 'This is all it gets you.'

14

'Are you sure about this?' Jack asked.

Denver paddled the raft on for one last stroke, then raised his hands and let them drift to a halt. He rolled on to his haunches with his arms outstretched for balance and confirmed that they were as close to the centre of the lake as they could be.

'Yeah,' he said. 'We've both seen what this much gold does to a man's mind and we got no assurance we'll ever get it to anyone who'll act responsibly. And besides, after being missing this long, who's to say who should really own it?'

Jack flashed a smile. 'I guess you got a point, but it's a shame to dump all of the gold.'

Denver raised his eyebrows and whistled under his breath.

'After everything you've been through and everything you've said, you ain't asking me to keep one or two bars back, are you?'

Jack winced then shivered. 'I guess I was. And that just proves you were right. Both my brothers let the gold persuade them to act stupidly, and despite everything that's happened, I still wouldn't take much persuading to be just as stupid.'

'In that case, you should throw the first bar.'

Jack nodded and took a bar from the pile in the middle of the raft. He took a deep breath, staring at the gold bar for long moments, the last rays of the sun dipping below the ridge lighting his face, then swung his hand to the side and dropped the bar.

The bar provided one last golden flash before it disappeared into the murky depths. Denver had no idea how deep the lake was, but he guessed it was too deep for anyone ever to get that far down.

But ever was a long time and one day the slow churning of the water would ensure that this gold would emerge again.

And then someone else could deal with the problems.

Denver threw the next bar into the water and he didn't even watch it disappear from view.

For the next half-hour each man sat solemnly facing the other and throwing gold bars over the side until the raft was bare.

Then they rowed back to dry land in silence.

While Jack prepared to head down the side of the lake to see if he could find his brother's body, Denver placed Fairborn's body over a spare horse. Then he piled the corrupt lawmen and Rico and his brothers — his gold — on the back of the wagon.

The two men faced each other one last time, each planning to head off in a different direction.

'You did the right thing,' Denver said. 'That gold wouldn't do you no good.'

'I know,' Jack said, sighing. 'Now I can go back to my old way of life, even if it is a bit more solitary.'

'And I wish you luck.'

Jack opened his mouth as if to say something, then closed it and tipped his hat. Still hunched, he led his horse away.

Denver watched him leave, frowning and offering a silent hope that Jack could reconcile himself to what he'd witnessed and done over the last few days, then he climbed on to the wagon and headed away from the lake.

As he gained higher land, Denver's frown turned to a smile and he delivered a rueful snort. He stopped and looked back along the side of the lake.

With his hand to his brow, he saw Jack's form, now small and distant as he headed around the lake. Jack had thought he'd been so careful in the way he'd slipped the single gold bar into his pocket when he thought Denver wasn't looking.

That was the trouble with gold — it burrowed its way into a man's mind and made him do things he'd never think himself capable of doing. But Denver was unconcerned and resolved to let him leave with the secreted bar.

After all, Denver had also taken a bar when Jack had had his back turned.

Denver turned the wagon and headed off on a circuitous, and, he hoped, seldom used route to Bluff Creek. There were still plenty of men out there looking to claim the bounty on his head. And with ten thousand dollars of bounty and several lawmen of supposedly good reputation lying dead in the wagon, ahead lay a battle to ensure he could cash in his bounty and prove he had acted correctly.

But as he trundled closer to Broken Rock Canyon, he consoled himself with one thought — if he failed, the gold bar they'd find on him was sure to raise a lot of curiosity.

MARSHAL LAW

Corba Sunman

Deputy Marshal Jed Law was sent to Buffalo Crossing to keep the peace; a bloody feud between two ranchers had already cost a man his life. But Law's real troubles started when he first set eyes on Julie Rutherford and her father Ben . . . Opposed by hard cases determined to wipe him out, he would be forced to shoot his way through. And worse was to come . . . Law would need his pistol loaded and ready to use until the last desperate shot.

HOT LEAD RANGE

Jack Holt

When an undercover agent going by the name of Bob Harker arrives in Sweetwater Valley, his task is to prevent a range war developing: the ruthless Butch Collins intends to claim the entire valley by forcing out his neighbours. One such neighbour is Frank Bateman — Harker's old boss when he was a Pinkerton detective. Harker manages to infiltrate the Collins outfit but, forced to take ever greater risks, could this be his final mission?

BADLANDERS

Ben Nicholas

The mining town of Sundown was running into chaos. When the sheriff faltered and shots sounded, hardcase miners took to the streets — fired up and ready for a showdown with anyone who stood in their way. Shane Carson was waiting for them at the jailhouse. Carson was no lawman, but he was a man on a mission — even if that meant standing alone against a murderous rabble. But could anybody hope to stand against such odds and live?